PRAISE FOR *CHANGE OF HEART*

"What a beautiful book! Readers will be haunted, as I am, by the characters who become so real and come to matter so much. I loved it."
—Danielle Steel, author of *First Sight* and *Matters of the Heart*

"I fell in love with Sharlie. I laughed with her, cried with her, and rooted for her. A lovely, tender story, moving and well told."
—Barbara Taylor Bradford, author of *Secrets from the Past* and *A Woman of Substance*

"A heartbreaker. Sally Mandel manages to say a good deal about love and loss and courage."
—*Publisher's Weekly*

"Takes off where Helen Van Slyke left off: wealthy Manhattan setting... sophisticated characters...an emotionally intense story line."
—*Library Journal*

"A book that seizes the heart. *Change of Heart* has all the ingredients of a good yarn, the sort we long for: I loved it."
—Nancy Milford, author of *Zelda*

PRAISE FOR *HEART AND SOUL*

"With wit and wisdom, Sally Mandel illuminates our deepest hopes and secret fears, showing us what matters most."
—Deborah Smith, author of *The Stone Flower Garden*

"Mandel displays her talent for establishing a strong female lead in an appealing millieu with an equally intriguing love interest."
—*Publisher's Weekly*

"A compelling drama...[with] fully dimensional characters."
—*Booklist*

PRAISE FOR *OUT OF THE BLUE*

"Funny, sad, tender, and triumphant."
—Kristin Hannah, author of *Fly Away* and *Summer Island*

"A novel of soaring spirit, steadfast love, and the willingness to reach for dreams...A wonderful book...filled with hope and faith."
—Luanne Rice, author of *The Lemon Orchard*

"Treat yourself to *Out of the Blue*, a joyful roller coaster of a story about love and hope and hanging on. A wonderful read!"
—Jennifer Crusie, author of *Welcome to Temptation*

Also by Sally Mandel
Change of Heart
Quinn
Heart and Soul
Out of the Blue
Portrait of a Married Woman
A Time to Sing

Diversion Books
A Division of Diversion Publishing Corp.
443 Park Avenue South, Suite 1004
New York, New York 10016
www.DiversionBooks.com

For more information, email info@diversionbooks.com

First Diversion Books edition September 2013.

Print ISBN: 978-1-62681-138-6
eBook ISBN: 978-1-626810-58-7

TAKE *me* BACK

SALLY MANDEL

DIVERSIONBOOKS

ACKNOWLEDGEMENTS

Writing *Take Me Back* was a personal triumph, but it never would have happened without the support of so many people. I was buoyed by the steadfast love of friends who put up with some pretty peculiar behavior until I really began to heal. Susan McClanahan and Martin Tandler phoned me on an almost daily basis to check up on me. Marva Ellis and Rose Austria guided me through the maze of domestic demands that seemed so overwhelming. Rob McQuilkin, my brilliant agent, treated the manuscript with attentive respect. Dr. Baruch Fishman armed me with specific exercises to chase away the demons. Ruona Bertaccini, my remedial cognitive therapist, worked with me for over a year to nudge my brain back into operation. Once the book was written, Carole Baron, Jamie Raab and Lydia Weaver legitimized its quality and made me feel like a writer again. And how can I ever thank Dr. Richard Friedman? He literally saved my life on several occasions when I simply could not face one more minute of hell. He insisted through it all that we would find a combination of medications that would work for me, and we did. My children, Ben and Sarah, and my husband, Barry, surrounded me with patient love always and never alerted me to their fears that I might never recover.

For Barry,

now more than ever.

INTRODUCTION
LETTER FROM A BROKEN BRAIN

In the months following my brain injury in February 2005, it became clear that I would never write another book. I had been a novelist for almost thirty years, during which time six of my books had been published. If I was not in the process of actually typing out the story, I was living with my characters, getting to know the details of their lives, what they wore, how they spoke to one another, what their most private secrets were. Sometimes I wondered whether my imagined world were not more "real" than reality. With a headful of characters I inevitably grew attached to, my life was always rich and colorful.

On that fateful winter day in Manhattan, I checked into the hospital for surgery on my hand. In many facilities, the operation is considered ambulatory, but my surgeon felt that I should remain overnight for pain control. My husband suggested that we hire a nurse to stay with me, but I told him that since I would not be undergoing general anesthesia, there was no need.

In the course of the night, a nurse checked my respiration rate, which was dangerously low. But rather than call immediately for help, he simply made the entry into my records and disappeared. By the time anyone saw me an hour or so later, I was unconscious—"coded blue". When I woke up in the ICU the next morning, a parade of medical personnel came by to express amazement that I was alive. No one knows exactly how I received the morphine overdose, but what *was* clear was that I had nearly died and that my brain, which had been deprived of oxygen for some period of time, would never entirely recover.

People who have undergone a traumatic event talk about

the "before" and "after" in their lives. Often, it takes only a splinter of time to hurl you from one into the other. Yet when I became conscious, I had no idea that I had just entered the "after" part of my life, no idea that I would never be the same.

What I remember most about those early days is the profound confusion. I had begun to perceive that things were "different," but could not figure out quite *how*. The rooms in my apartment seemed changed, the view out the window peculiar. I could stare ahead for long periods of time with no thoughts, just a vague sense that there was nothing but a hollow space between my ears where echoes of thoughts and memories made an incoherent murmur. I had a CT scan, a PET scan, an MRI. I underwent hours of neurological testing. Finally, the diagnosis confirmed irreparable damage to my left frontal lobe. In my mind, I pictured a dent there, like the evidence left behind after an automobile collision.

At each of the many doctor visits thereafter I was required to fill out a form. Always, there was the blank line for "Profession." It had been a long road to achieving the right to call myself a writer, and it had always given me a little throb of pleasure to scribble it down in the blank space. "What am I now," I thought, "an ex-writer"?

Then I would be called in to see that day's doctor and he would tell me that after six months, or nine months, or a year, I would reach the apex of my recovery and that I should expect no more improvement thereafter. The stranger who had moved into my familiar skin would never disappear.

There was guilt. I would look at pictures in the newspaper of soldiers who had suffered brain damage in Iraq. Some were paralyzed, or had lost their ability to speak. I told myself that I was lucky. I could so easily have died. The conviction that I might be over-reacting, however, only served to send me deeper into despair and so, like many people who suffer brain injury, I plummeted into a profound depression. I thought about suicide every day. Sometimes, killing myself was the only image I could focus on. I imagined with longing the nothingness of oblivion.

My psychopharmacologist worked with me for more than

a year to find the effective combination of drugs that would, without turning me into a total zombie, diminish the constant yearning for self-destruction. I could tell from the way my family and friends looked at me that I was certainly a *partial* zombie. They addressed me as they would a baffled child, which is pretty much what I was.

After I got the cast off my hand, my daughter and I went to an eco-lodge in Belize. She was in her early twenties at the time, and I suppose I was thinking that I was "taking her" on vacation as I had so many times before. In fact, she took charge of me, from the moment I got lost in the airport to her returning me to my room. We had adjoining cabins, but I simply could not keep track of where I was supposed to be or when. I showed up at mealtimes too early or too late. I wandered aimlessly around the hotel grounds. At night, before my daughter went to bed, she stuck post-its on my bedside table telling me at what time I was supposed to meet her for breakfast and listing our activities for the morning—separately, so that there was not too much information on any one scrap. It soon became clear that I needed reminders for everything: set alarm, file nails, wash out socks, show up for an activity, and so on.

What I remember most about that trip, though, is sitting in a garden seat beside my gentle warden, swinging idly back and forth, just talking quietly. It was peaceful there, with one person I loved and trusted, a person I could relate to. I clung to that healing memory, and still do.

Back in Manhattan, I found that I could not understand the implications of red light/green light at street corners and trained myself to follow the crowd at intersections. I got lost in my neighborhood because I could not "see" familiar landmarks. The tailor, whom I had visited countless times in over thirty years, had simply disappeared. I walked back and forth, back and forth, before the shop inexplicably reappeared. This inability to "see" applied to items around the house as well. I could not find my glasses even when I was staring directly at them. It was always so startling when they would materialize hours later in the exact spot that I had searched before. I came to realize that what I saw—or didn't see—could not be trusted.

I could not tolerate bright light or noise. I had to leave restaurants and sit on the curb outside, hoping that an ambulance or fire truck with their excruciating sirens would not pass by. I wore sunglasses indoors against the ever present glare. Even now, years later, how I love a rainy day!

Although some of my symptoms have eased, many remain problematic. My short-term memory, for example, is shot. My husband recounts places we recently visited, social occasions we attended, people we spent an evening with. It's all news to me. We call the place in my head where all this stuff must surely be stored the "Black Hole."

My vocabulary continues to be eccentric and elusive. I have trouble grasping the right word and I say things like, "Have you ever been to Niagara Farms?" Then I'll try to correct myself: "No, that's not it. Have you ever been to Niagara Farms?" It may come out right after a few more tries or it may not. Or I'll ask, "Can you pick up a bottle of wrinkle?" If I cannot retrieve the word, "water," I'll talk around it: "You know, it's in a lake, you drink it, it's what rain is…" Even when the answer is given, I often still cannot say it aloud.

Numbers continue to mystify me. The first time I tried to play bridge, I tossed a card out of my hand to make a trick with the three others on the table. I stared at them in bewilderment. I tried to make my brain "move" but it was simply stuck in neutral. "I don't know what they mean," I told my husband. His eyes filled with tears.

After countless hours of daily rehab, I have improved in understanding things numerical, especially if I can see them. Listening to a chain of numbers being read to me over the phone makes my head hurt. I may have to ask for a confirmation number three times, and "slowly, please," before I can manage to write it down. "9" still reads as the letter "n", and "7" as "s".

Reading presents a challenge. During rehab, I began with articles in the New York Times. My rehab specialist would select one and ask me to read the first paragraph to myself. She would then inquire what it meant. I would inevitably answer, "I have no idea." She would explain how to take the first sentence apart, a few words at a time. When I understood those, I could move on to the next phrase. Using this system, I would usually be able to absorb the meaning, but one small article could take half an hour of analysis. It was agonizing how quickly I could lose all memory of a sentence when I had struggled over it just minutes before.

When I was a child, bedtime meant hiding under the covers with my book and a flashlight. Ever since, I have always read before falling asleep. It was a delicious transporting time before drifting off. After The Event, however, it became an ordeal. I would read a paragraph several times through, using my new technique. That worked all right—eventually, I could put away two or three pages. But the next night, I would open to the following page and could remember nothing of what I had read before. And so… back to the beginning. It was a painstaking, frustrating process. But it was the only way to learn, once again, how to read.

All of this is a partial explanation of why I knew, without question or doubt, that I would never write a novel again. If I could not even read a book, how could I possibly expect myself to write one?

And yet…

You may be wondering what the attached pile of pages following this letter represents. I can tell you: years of hard work every day, going through childish exercises with my rehab specialist, and finally graduating to doing many of them on my own. Reading and more reading, and never letting up. Because it is all too easy to slip back. Fighting discouragement and depression with medication and positive reinforcement from my always optimistic psychopharmacologist, my patient and loving family, my loyal friends. Closing my ears to certain physicians I consulted who kept telling me I'd already achieved what I could reasonably expect. Trying to finish the *New York Times* crossword every day, watching Jeopardy. Daring to make my first solo drive at the wheel of our car. Summoning the courage to take a trip by myself, getting lost in the airport but controlling my panic.

Learning to make lists for everything and trying to remember to take those lists with me. And to read them. Accepting that I would become exhausted every day simply from trying to make sense out of the words assaulting me via telephone, television, people behind the grocery counter, ordinary conversations. Respecting the need to shut myself off from the world in a dark room for an hour every afternoon so that I might be ready for the battle that is the rest of the day. That I am first to leave a celebratory event, as at my own daughter's wedding, when I become overwhelmed by my own emotions and by the crowd. Accepting that I will lose friends who cannot understand that while I may appear normal, I am, in fact, forever changed. That I will forget promises and lose track of commitments.

And so I confronted, as best I could, the challenges necessary to lead a semblance of a normal life, which, for me, includes the act of writing. It was a leap of faith. For a long time, the concept was unimaginable. But one evening over dinner, my husband asked, "How about trying to write again?"

I have learned to pay attention to this man I've spent nearly the whole of my life with when he looks at me in a particularly penetrating way. His life has changed along with mine, of course. He has become expert at reading my face for signs of confusion or distress. Not only does he know my weaknesses, he usually figures out before I do when I need to adjust my medication or take a nap. Talk about love. I can't begin to tell you—he has kept me afloat through it all. But write?

I stared at him as if his hair had caught on fire and explained that in order to write each sentence of a novel, you must recall everything you've written before. I couldn't remember what I had for breakfast. It wasn't going to happen.

"What about a short story?" he asked.

"I've never written a short story in my life," I said.

"So?" he said.

"Hm," I thought.

And then, after many months, the first chapter of *Take Me Back* was born, the one introducing Lily Adams. It is a hard-won twenty-six pages long, with at least a hundred pages of notes to support its creation. After Lily's debut, I was surprised that I could not stop thinking about another character in the story, her granddaughter, Amy. Maybe I ought to try experimenting with her, I thought. I liked the result. After that there were Lily's daughter, Stella, and William, and Simon. Lo and behold, one day after years of trial and error, it turned out that I had written … a novel.

The morning I wrote the final word, I burst into tears, I must report, and fell down on my knees. I'm not a religious person, understand; this was totally a reflexive thing. I simply had to express my gratitude somehow.

So that's my story. That's why this book is so different from my others, born as it was from a profoundly grueling and intimate experience. It was immensely satisfying.

It was my beloved son, a surgeon, who first pored through the hundred pages of documentation of my hospital stay in order to determine exactly what had happened to me, and to bring to light the negligence that had left me permanently damaged. Along with being the kind of doctor who would never allow such a thing to occur on his watch, he is protective of his Mom. The guy still holds my hand when we walk down the street together.

Anyway, he phoned me a while ago and asked, "So, Mom, are you going to write another one?"

"I don't have a single idea," I replied. "Nope, not a one."

And, as it happened, the very next day, Ellie Taft strolled into my head. She's been there ever since. In some ways, I feel that I already know her better than I do myself. But maybe, as I write her story, she will help me understand and accept the unfamiliar person that I have now become.

MRS. ADAMS

Lily: 1992

The first time Mrs. Adams heard the voices she turned up her hearing aid. But no, there was no one in the room, no one outside the door. She dismissed the sounds as some dysfunction of the apparatus; sometimes things penetrated loud and clear, other times everything seemed filtered through flannel. Often when the voices spoke, she was not wearing it at all. At first there had been only fragments, like unrelated syllables, but these days a low murmur might last as much as a minute, with certain words that she could make out quite clearly: *new dress*; *Sundays*; *philosophy*. She was certain that she'd heard the word *Studebaker*, for instance, and once even the phrase *such a good soul*. It seemed that the low babble came from somewhere over her right shoulder. There was a sliver of light there, too, as if a door were ajar. If she blinked, it disappeared. She never mentioned this to anyone, not even Alice. It didn't frighten her; she just found it distracting, puzzling and even intriguing.

The day that she had her spell, she was sitting as usual in her favorite chair by the window, working the *Times* crossword puzzle. There were some fine antiques in the room—a Colonial bureau, a Persian rug, a few pieces of nineteenth century Chinese porcelain, one of which Mrs. Adams used to hold M&M's in case her granddaughter turned up unexpectedly. There was a wall hanging of Chinese ancestors over the sofa brought back by her missionary father and a Tiffany lamp beside her on the table. The room had the pleasant air of beat-up gentility, the early morning sun casting a warm glow onto the newspaper Mrs.

Adams held on her lap.

The tremor in her hand made holding the pencil difficult, but Amy had somewhere unearthed a special kind with a rubber grip that improved things a little. The Parkinson's had announced itself dramatically by tripping her up on a short flight of stairs and sending her tumbling, thankfully with nothing broken, just a few nasty bruises. Reluctantly, she began to use a cane, which compensated somewhat for her increasingly lurching gait. The disease thereafter had crept up slowly, only gradually impairing her functions over the course of a decade. She measured its impact at least in part by the expression on Amy's face when she made her sporadic visits.

"Gran, your hands are shaking a lot more. Isn't there anything you can take for that?" She still wore her hair tied back in a ponytail, just as she had when she was a little girl.

Mrs. Adams smiled. "It's a blessing in disguise, dear. I do believe I've written my last birthday card." The sadness in her granddaughter's face had thrown such a shadow over the old woman's heart that she had to clasp her trembling hands together and hide them in her lap.

Alice showed up at ten o'clock sharp, as always. She hung up her jacket and went to clear Mrs. Adams' TV tray of dishes. "Morning, Mrs. A," she said, inspecting the remains of breakfast to assure herself that Mrs. Adams was eating enough. Skin and bones, she was. Alice held the juice glass up to the light and looked quizzically at Mrs. Adams. It was supposed to be coated with a film of a sweet chocolate protein drink to help keep weight on the old woman. "Ensure," it was called, though Mrs. Adams referred to it as "Endure." No film this morning.

"Champagne," Mrs. Adams explained. "Left over from Charlie's birthday party last night."

"For breakfast?" Alice asked.

"I wasn't going to let it go to waste," Mrs. Adams protested. "Besides, champagne makes a lovely complement to cornflakes. Tell me, what's it like outside?"

"The daffodils are all out along the sidewalk."

"It's about time," Mrs. Adams said. "Imagine, waiting until

the end of April for a daffodil."

The apartment complex had been built during the 1940s to accommodate returning soldiers and their families. In those days, the place was teeming with children. Eventually, the original families moved into nearby houses. Then, as their children grew up and moved away, many of the parents returned to take up residence in the same apartments they had occupied in their youth. Sunny Hills, as it was called now, had gained a reputation as a comfortable place for the elderly with a decent hospital in nearby Syracuse with reliable access to caretakers. Alice, who'd previously worked as a hostess in a local restaurant, discovered an affinity for old folks. They appreciated her quiet efficiency and her genuine interest in their pasts. From Alice's point of view, these people provided a window back into history. So long as they weren't mean and didn't require professional nursing care beyond her capacities, she enjoyed her work. Mrs. Adams, though, was by far her favorite. The old woman had been educated abroad and spoke three or four languages. She always told Alice, "Spend the money on good goods and you'll never be sorry." She had a ladylike way about her, a delicacy in her manner that threw into relief a certain ribald tendency that never failed to floor Alice. This morning, for example.

"Charlie's asked me out on a jaunt," Mrs. Adams said, leaning to pat the seat beside her for Alice to sit.

Handing Mrs. Adams the morning's *New York Times*, Alice settled in and opened her container of coffee. "What sort of a jaunt?"

"To use his car for intercourse."

Alice gaped. Mrs. Adams was smiling at her in that sweet way she had.

"I know, but it was my hearing aid. The battery quit on me and I guess I missed a syllable or two," the old woman went on. "What he wanted was to *cruise* in his golf cart *out on the course.*"

Alice laughed.

"Anyway, I'm a little long in the tooth for that kind of behavior. But a little spin in the sunshine? So long as Charlie doesn't put us in the ditch, that sounds just fine to me."

"Well, be careful," Alice said. "We may never see you alive again."

Charlie Hartwick was famous for polishing off his wives. He'd had three so far, and they'd all died within ten years of marrying him.

"Oh, I'll be safe so long as I stay single." Mrs. Adams glanced at the front page of the newspaper. War, lies and mayhem, it was always the same. So discouraging. Though it didn't help that she felt a bit out of sorts this morning. A touch of spring fever, perhaps, or was it the champagne? Everything seemed just a little out of reach. "I'll tell you what, Alice. Let's look at an album. I'm not sure I have the brains for a puzzle."

Alice set her coffee aside and went to the bookshelf. Looking through Mrs. Adams' photograph albums was always a treat. "Which one?" she asked.

"Why don't you bring over the red one? It's got everybody in it, all mixed up together. Shall we go sit on the couch?"

"Sure," Alice said, setting the album on the coffee table in front of the sofa. When she turned around, Mrs. Adams was staring hard at a spot on the wall to her right, a peculiar look on her face.

The voices were accompanied by the shattering of glass this time, as if a waiter had overturned a tray. Then there was laughter. The crack of light widened for just an instant before fading away.

"Are you all right?" Alice was asking.

"Oh, I'm fine," Mrs. Adams said, with Alice's help easing herself out of the chair and shuffling over to the sofa. "Aim that lamp right here onto the pictures, will you?" Her eyes were still pretty good, especially after she'd had the cataracts removed, but she always liked light, the more the better, sunlight especially. It was a wonder she'd never developed a melanoma considering the amount of time she spent out in the sun over the course of her life.

She flipped open the album. "Hah! Well, there we are," she said. A girl in her mid-twenties stood leaning against a man beside the steps to an airplane. They were all dressed up in the way people were for airplane trips back in those days. It had always saddened her how Stella would head off to the airport for one of her escapades in a pair of jeans. Flying on an airplane had once called for hose and high heels.

"That's your husband, isn't it?" Alice asked.

"Yes. William. Look at that airplane. One step removed from the Wright brothers."

"He's very handsome," Alice said. She was curious about Mr. Adams, had heard he was "difficult," had a bit of a short fuse. Still, she liked the way he stood in the photo, cocky almost, with one arm draped possessively around his young wife.

"I suppose," Mrs. Adams said matter-of-factly. "I've been told he had what you'd call sex appeal."

When she met William at her cousin's wedding, she had been half engaged to another man—a very kind person, a banker who went on to run a big insurance company. But William had pursued her just the same, no regard for proprieties, thinking nothing of barging right into her family's home out in Princeton, interrupting their Thanksgiving dinner, and insisting on speaking with her father. She realized many years later, when she was old enough to know herself better, that it had been his persistence that won the day. He wanted her more than the banker did, it was a simple as that, and Mrs. Adams yielded to the stronger force, never mind what she herself felt. The thing about William, he was never boring. You never knew what was going to happen when he walked into the room. He had a disturbing animal grace about him, a wicked smile, and he could make her laugh like nobody ever had or would.

"He died too young," Alice said.

"Fifteen years ago," Mrs. Adams said, turning the album page. "He was the kind that burned out early." William had just pulled off the road and had a quiet heart attack. Not at all the dramatic ending she might have predicted for him. She didn't think she would ever stop crying.

"Here she is," Mrs. Adams said, pointing at a slightly out-of-focus photograph of herself across from a young girl in early adolescence. The pair was sitting at a restaurant table with a floral centerpiece. "Those were plastic flowers," Mrs. Adams remarked. "Such a funny old place. The waiter, I remember, wore a tuxedo but he served wine from a screw-top bottle. It said 'Starch du Jour' on the menu."

Mrs. Adams had loved many people over the course of her eighty-one years, but with just one exception, her affections always suffered from the strain of ambivalence. She admired her father for his intellect and rigorous morality, but he intimidated her. Her mother had dispensed maternal favors dutifully but without warmth. Stella, well, she was a constant worry, with her wild moods and frightening need to travel; she never quite got used to Stella's being called away to some godforsaken place for her work. Where was it now, Honduras? Love was a complicated business, all right.

Except when it came to Amy. When Stella had gone into labor with Amy down in New York City, Mrs. Adams made a point of keeping her bridge date. It was the only time in her life that she could remember yearning for a tranquilizer, not to mention the only time she had ever drawn a hand that totaled twenty-four points. Fortunately, her partner wound up playing the slam. Mrs. Adams had gone into the powder room and sat on the edge of the bathtub rocking back and forth, the sound of her thumping heart seeming to bounce off the marble surfaces around her.

When Stella and Amy got out of the hospital, she'd gone down to help. William wasn't happy with her leaving. He never liked an empty house, even though much of the time he was off doing the Lord-knew-what with his chums. But not even William's displeasure could stand in the way. Stella's husband had shown no sign of domestic skills and a new mother always needed an extra pair of hands while she recovered. So Mrs. Adams took care of the laundry and the cooking while Stella had a chance to get used to her baby daughter. In the night, however, Mrs. Adams let Stella sleep and got to feed the baby herself. Those hours still shone in Mrs. Adams' memory as some of the most precious of her life. Rocking Amy, she would look down into her tiny face, overwhelmed suddenly by such profound love that tears rolled down her cheeks.

Raising their own child, Mrs. Adams had always kept a respectful distance from her needs. As she had been taught by her own mother, responsible parenting meant not giving in to the protests of a child who simply needed to take a nap, who had been fed quite enough, who had cried long enough over a scraped knee. And so she had steeled herself against her own impulse to spoil her daughter with hugs and kisses. But with Amy, she had felt no such obligation. Let Stella struggle with building Amy's character. Mrs. Adams was the grandmother, and as such, she had a perfect right to indulge Amy without restraint.

Mrs. Adams remembered any number of dinners out with her grandchild. In fact, the events still seemed fresh and immediate in her mind, unlike other memories—her own wedding, for example—which were somehow out of focus, like the images on a television with poor reception. Mrs. Adams peered at the photograph and remembered that there had been a birthday party at a nearby table that evening, the guest of honor a little girl of ten or so. Fat and wearing unbecoming glasses, she was flanked by two pretty friends who leaned across her to chatter and giggle.

"They only came for the restaurant," Amy complained to Mrs. Adams.

Meanwhile, the mother of the birthday girl kept up a frantic patter, a desperately festive smile plastered on her face. The birthday girl, for her part, just stared down at her plate.

"We've got to do something," Amy said. "What can we *do*?"

They looked at one another, misty-eyed, and laughed at their mutual susceptibility.

"Let's buy her a drink," Mrs. Adams said.

"Oh yes!" Amy cried. She twisted around in her chair and beckoned the waiter over. He stood inquiringly beside Mrs. Adams, who nodded at Amy.

"Could you please send the girl over there a Shirley Temple?" Amy asked. "And could you put extra cherries in it?"

"With our compliments," Mrs. Adams added.

"Yes!" Amy said. "With our *compliments*!"

Mrs. Adams let her hand drift across the photograph as if caressing it. She and Amy had watched the drink arrive, and then the bewilderment, the explanation from the waiter, and finally the flush on the little girl's face as she smiled across the room at them. Amy and Mrs. Adams had lifted their own glasses. "Happy birthday!" they called out. "Happy birthday to you!"

"Isn't she coming soon?" Alice asked. "Amy?"

Mrs. Adams looked up from the album, willing herself back into the present. "Yes. Friday." There was a tinkling sound near her right ear, like the distant ripple of piano keys, and she could even make out the tune: a leisurely rendition of "I Remember You." She closed her eyes and dozed off. When she woke up, Alice was handing her a cup of tea.

After lunch, Charlie knocked and poked his head in the door. Nobody ever bothered to lock up at Sunny Hills.

"In?" he asked.

"Oh, yes, Charlie—come in," Mrs. Adams said. Alice smirked at her but Mrs. Adams pretended not to notice.

Mrs. Adams had known him since the early years of her marriage. He and his then wife, Margaret, had been part of the same gang. They raised their kids together, picnicked in the summers by the creek, threw cocktail parties, and played golf. Slim and athletic, he was still handsome at eighty-two, with a full head of dark hair. Charlie had always been a snazzy dresser and today, in his yellow and melon plaid sports jacket with a yellow polo shirt, he was no exception.

"You look like the sunrise, Charlie," Mrs. Adams said. "Sit down, won't you?"

"No," Charlie said. "I came to whisk you away on my trusty steed."

"I don't know if I'm much up to being whisked," Mrs. Adams said. She knew he was referring to his much-beloved golf cart. Charlie could be seen driving around the property most every day, even in a drizzle. They had taken his car keys away after he backed through the closed doors of the garage in his sedan, but so far he had managed to protect his authority over the cart. Mrs. Adams shifted her weight in the chair, testing her legs, which seemed in no hurry to obey instructions. In fact, she felt a bit queer all over.

"Take a look out your window," Charlie said, stepping over to the curtain and pulling it aside. "What a day!"

Mrs. Adams squinted at the locust tree on the lawn outside, bathed in sunshine, its buds just about to burst open. It had been a day like this at least thirty years before when Stella's friend Deke showed up outside the house on a brand-new Harley-Davidson. Stella and Mrs. Adams were admiring it when suddenly Deke handed Mrs. Adams a helmet. "Put it on. We're going for a ride." Mrs. Adams had protested with a laugh, but Deke helped her on with the helmet. "You're my first passenger," he said. A few of the neighbors had heard the racket and had wandered out onto their yards to watch. Mrs. Adams settled onto the seat behind Deke, and off they went with a roar. She could hear Stella whooping.

Mrs. Adams knew how it would smell outside, the earth coming back to life after the snow's final melt.

"Alice," she said. "I think I'll need my down coat." Charlie took her arm to lift her out of the chair.

"You don't weigh much more than a hummingbird," he said.

As soon as she stepped out the door, Mrs. Adams took a deep breath. "*My*, that air is bracing!" she exclaimed.

Charlie drove slowly on level ground along the sidewalk that circled the complex. Mrs. Adams looked this way and that, shading her eyes in the bright sun. There was a blustery wind, but it was just posturing. She wished that Charlie could drive the golf cart up into the stately hills that undulated gracefully across upstate New York. She used to love to go up there with William, loved to park by the side of the road among the neat dairy farms and unspoiled woodlands. You could see all the way to the Adirondack foothills from up there.

Charlie turned onto the gravel path that entered the woods just north of the apartments. There was still sun under the trees. Still, Mrs. Adams drew her coat around her as the cart bumped and lurched on its way until they reached a clearing where benches had been set out by a lone picnic table.

"Come, let's sit," Charlie said, turning off the ignition.

"Trilliums," Mrs. Adams said, pointing. "I haven't seen those purple ones in years." They rested on the bench in silence a moment. "Isn't life just simply glorious?" she said finally.

"Yes, because you're in it," Charlie answered.

Mrs. Adams gave him an impatient little nudge. "And you're full of applesauce."

Charlie took her hand. "I'm going to ask you again, Lily."

She looked into that face full of entreaty. "Oh, Charlie. You know what I'm going to say."

"Where there's life, there's hope," he said. "It's been at least six months."

"But why would you ever want to marry an old crone like me? You know I'm going downhill. You'd wind up taking care of me night and day …."

"I *want* to take care of you, Lily. It would be a privilege to take care of you."

She thought about his first wife's long illness. Charlie had been a saint. Some people were born caretakers, she supposed, but Mrs. Adams had no desire to be on the receiving end of some man's charity. Alice was just fine—perfect, even—a no-nonsense presence who required nothing in return for her services except good manners and a regular paycheck.

"Once upon a time you gave me reason to hope," Charlie went on. "I haven't brought it up until now only because somehow it seemed … indelicate."

Mrs. Adams knew perfectly well what was coming and withdrew her hand.

"You kissed me, Lily," he said.

"That was forty years ago!"

"Yes, and it was an important kiss," Charlie said.

For her as well, in a way. She had been so angry with William that night. He had returned late from a business trip the week before, and as always, she had unpacked his suitcase for him the next morning. When she removed one of his golf shoes, out fell a pair of black lace panties. There had been tears, slammed doors, an icy silence. The following Sunday, there was a party at the country club. Mrs. Adams drank three glasses of wine—one drink over her limit. Charlie danced with her a few times, and when he drew her into the library and leaned down for a kiss, she had thought, *Oh why not?* only wishing that William had been there to witness the little infidelity. From that time forward, the kiss became a kind of armor against her husband. When he hurt or angered her, she thought to herself, *Yes, all right, but I kissed Charlie Hartwick.*

"It was just a cocktail flirtation," she said.

"You're all lit up, Lily," Charlie said, taking her hand again. "You're like a candle in the dark. I want you with me all the time."

That was the last thing Mrs. Adams heard before there was the roar that overtook her ears, and then the blackness. When she was next aware, she was on her bed. Alice was removing her shoes.

"Charlie went for the doctor," Alice said.

Mrs. Adams lifted her head a little to test the waters. The room swam. "I must have had a spell," she said.

"I'll say. You passed out cold."

Mrs. Adams began to remember the trip back on the cart. Charlie's arm had pinned her to him, keeping her secure.

"I'm getting Mary to stay with you tonight," Alice said.

"Is that really necessary?" Mrs. Adams asked. And yet she was pleased. Alice's daughter reminded her of her own granddaughter, though they looked nothing alike. Mary was powerfully built, almost manly, not at all slender like Amy. They both had a fresh smell about them, though, like lavender but not at all cloying. Perhaps they used the same shampoo.

The doctor, whom Mrs. Adams regarded as practically a teenager (a know-it-all as well, although she'd never say so), pronounced her well enough, though a little dehydrated and probably overtired. He recommended twenty-four hours of bed rest. Then, sometime after midnight, Mrs. Adams' temperature began to climb. By morning, it was 102 degrees, and she had developed a cough.

"You just don't like spring, do you?" Alice complained when she came to relieve Mary. Last year this time, Mrs. Adams had contracted a strep throat from her bridge partner. It took three weeks to get it under control.

"When did you say Amy was due?" Mrs. Adams asked. It was a struggle to talk. She felt as if she had a large furry animal lodged in her chest.

"Day after next," Alice said. "Friday. Would you like me to phone her? Or your daughter?"

Mrs. Adams waved her hand impatiently. "You girls make such a fuss over a little fever."

"Do you remember talking to me in the middle of the night?" Mary asked. She smoothed Mrs. Adams' blankets with her large practical hands.

"No," Mrs. Adams said. "I slept like a log."

Mrs. Adams had always awakened during the night, usually to read for an hour or so. She regarded her interrupted sleep as perfectly restful and refreshing. "It's just left over from waiting up for Stella to come home," she had explained. "Or William."

"Well, you were chatty, all right," Mary said. "First you asked me if I heard the music. Then a little later, you said they were serving hors d'oeuvres."

"Sounds like a good party to me," Alice said.

Mrs. Adams was quiet. She must have stepped into that room with the voices. She wished she could remember.

She was unable to eat anything all day. Alice pressed her to take a few sips of her "Endure," which was tough going. With each passing hour, Mrs. Adams' chest felt heavier. It was difficult to breathe, but she slept most of the time. Then, at five o'clock, the doctor showed up again.

He sat beside her on the bed. "*Lily!*" he shouted at her. Alice scowled as Mrs. Adams' eyes flew open. "Let's get a look at you!" His collar was too big around his neck, as if he hadn't yet grown into his clothes. Mrs. Adams peered at him through a fog of fever. His face was pink and round, a face that would never be taken seriously. She tried to give him an encouraging smile but felt that her effort fell short. She was so tired.

The doctor listened to her chest for some time. She fell asleep before he was finished; he had to wake her up again to deliver the verdict. "You've got a touch of pneumonia, Lily. We need to send you to the hospital for just a few days until we can clear it up."

Mrs. Adams looked at him balefully. "I don't think so," she said.

"Oh, yes, indeed," the doctor said, squeezing her hand. "And a ride in the ambulance, too."

"No more hospitals," Mrs. Adams said.

"Nonsense," he said. "We'll have you out of there in a jiffy, right as rain."

"Doctor," Mrs. Adams said, lifting herself up on her pillows. "I'll recover right here in my own bed, thank you. If I should curl up my toes and die, I won't hold you accountable." She fell back against her pillow and began to cough.

"Could you get a nurse over here?" Alice asked him. "You can hook up an IV for the antibiotics. I see other folks here in the complex do that."

"These people don't know what's best for them," the doctor grumbled. "I wouldn't be surprised if she's beginning to suffer from dementia."

"She's got every marble she was born with," Alice retorted.

Have I become invisible all of a sudden? Mrs. Adams wondered.

The doctor sighed. "I'll see what I can do about a nurse."

Her temperature did not go down. She lay with an IV in her arm and plastic tubing in her nose to provide extra oxygen. The doctor had ordered twenty-four hour nursing, but just the same Alice dropped by. She knew Mrs. Adams' ways, her favorite foods, and the television programs she liked if she got strong enough to go into the other room to watch. Charlie came to see her, too. He stood next to the bed and wrung his hands.

"Oh, Lily, look what I've done to you," he said.

"Don't be absurd," she said.

"I never should have taken you out on such a windy day."

"It was a beautiful day and I'll never forget it. Those trilliums." She closed her eyes. "Or trillia? Which is it?"

"May I just sit by you for a while? I won't make you talk."

"All right," she said.

He settled in the little cane chair in the corner, dwarfing it with his lanky body.

"You're my knight, Charlie," she murmured after a while.

He had thought she was asleep. "What was that?" he asked her.

"My knight, I said. That's you."

Charlie struggled to find his voice, and croaked out a muffled thank you. Finally the nurse came in to banish him.

Mrs. Adams drifted in and out of fever dreams, mostly pleasant and populated with a cast of thousands. She rode on a roller coaster with her father. He was wearing his collar. Though that was more of a memory than a dream. Her father was a thrill seeker. She wondered sometimes if he hadn't chosen to be a missionary simply to get paid for traipsing off into uncharted territory. He had complete confidence that God would protect him, though her mother liked to protest that he pushed God to the limit and beyond. There had been that incident with the tribe in New Guinea. "You're just like me, Lil," he had told his daughter more than once. "You're not afraid of anything."

That was not entirely true. She had been afraid of William on occasion, of anyone in a rage, really, even strangers. They felt physically dangerous, as if their personal shrapnel might explode right into her. From time to time, she thought she might be afraid of God as well, but the fact was Mrs. Adams wasn't at all sure she believed in him. There had been entirely too much religion in her early years, pulling the curtains on Sundays and reading from the Bible until she felt like flinging it across the room. Certainly, she resented any force that could have allowed Stella to suffer painful ear infections as a baby. What kind of omnipotent spirit would permit such suffering in an innocent? And then there was the lost one. No, Mrs. Adams had no patience with that sort of cruelty. She preferred to believe in the human spirit, that it was precious and indestructible.

"What day is it?" she asked the nurse.

"Thursday," the woman answered. She was gentle, with a

pretty accent, maybe Indian, or Pakistani.

"Ah, still Thursday," Mrs. Adams said. Her room looked distorted, as if she were peering at it through the wrong end of binoculars.

That evening, they started pestering her about a proper hospital bed.

"Since you *won't* go to St. Joseph's," the doctor said in an injured tone.

"We can make you so much more comfortable in a hospital bed," the nurse said. This one spoke too loud and seemed always to be chewing on something.

Mrs. Adams smiled a little. She knew whose comfort they were talking about. "You wouldn't bully an old woman," she said.

They moved to the other side of the room and conferred together. The binocular vision rendered them oddly small from where she lay, but her hearing aid was having one of its moments of clarity, and their voices were very distinct. She heard the nurse ask the doctor about trying a different antibiotic.

"Just make sure she doesn't dislodge that oxygen tube," he said. "It's the only thing keeping her alive."

Amy arrived on Friday afternoon. Alice was in the sitting room with the newspaper, making an attempt to do the crossword puzzle.

"Gran napping?" Amy asked.

Dropping her heavy backpack to the floor, Amy was tall and slim in her jeans and cable knit sweater. Her pale hair was pulled back in a ponytail, making her look younger than twenty-eight. At Alice's expression, Amy's features tensed, like an animal in a forest catching the first scent of fire. "What's wrong?"

"She's got a respiratory infection. Pneumonia."

A groove appeared between Amy's eyebrows.

"Hasn't responded to the antibiotics yet," Alice went on. "Then again, it was the same way last spring, with her throat. It just took some time for the medication to work."

Amy tiptoed to the bedroom and peeked in, then turned

back to Alice with a face almost accusatory. "There's a nurse!"

"Oh, honey, she's tough. It'll be all right."

"Don't *bullshit* me, Alice."

The older woman couldn't help smiling. The word choice differed, but the tone was unmistakably that of her grandmother. Amy went into the bedroom and pulled the cane chair up next to the bed.

Feeling Amy's hand on hers, Mrs. Adams opened her eyes, and seeing it was Amy, smiled broadly. "It's Friday."

"Why didn't you call me, Gran?"

"I knew you were coming."

"What about Mom?"

"I'm not fetching her back from Belize or wherever."

"Do you feel very awful?"

"Well, I do have an emu nesting in my chest. And I don't suppose I look very glamorous with this tube stuck in my nose." There was laughter and a smattering of applause off to the right. She ignored it and kept her focus trained on Amy.

"What?" Amy asked, seeing her grandmother's eyes flicker.

Mrs. Adams shook her head. "Now, tell me what's happening with the book."

"Oh shit," Amy said. "Another rejection."

"Did you change the scene by the dam?"

"No."

"Good," Mrs. Adams said. "It's what holds the second half together."

"I got a job as a receptionist at a law firm," Amy said.

Mrs. Adams frowned.

"I know, but it's a pay check."

"If you'd just be sensible," Mrs. Adams said. Amy was so proud when it came to money.

"You know how I feel about that, Gran," Amy said. "It's enough that you have faith in me."

"Well, you're just lucky I'm too pooped to argue," Mrs. Adams said.

"Do you want to sleep for a little?" Amy asked.

"Are you staying?"

"Yes."

"Then I'll sleep."

A stab of pain under her ribs woke Mrs. Adams. The night nurse was on, so she must have been sleeping a while.

"You've been moaning," the nurse said, leaning over her. "Let me give you something for the pain."

"Will it make me muzzy?" Mrs. Adams asked.

"It'll help you rest."

"All right, just don't make me muzzy." And then she drifted away again. When she awoke, Amy was beside her, her hair loose around her face.

"Did you get any sleep on that awful couch?" Mrs. Adams asked her.

"Like a rock," Amy said. There was a sudden report as the window shade snapped open. Mrs. Adams startled.

"It's okay," Amy said. "Just the shade."

Archy and Mehitabel, the two bedroom shades named long ago by Mrs. Adams, had the habit of rewinding for no discernable reason. Amy had always taken their whimsical behavior for granted, and it wasn't until she studied American literature at college that she discovered who Archy and Mehitabel actually were.

"Which one?" Gran asked.

"Archy," Amy said.

"Oh, that Archy." Mrs. Adams shifted a little in her bed.

"How are you, Gran?"

"Fit as a fiddle." She coughed and put her hand to her chest. It felt as if all her ribs had cracked. Amy's face told her that she looked as dreadful as she felt. "Talk to me," she said.

Amy took Mrs. Adams' hand and put its soft dry skin to her cheek. "Did you know that my very first memory is of you?" Amy asked. Mrs. Adams heard the quaver in her granddaughter's voice and pretended she hadn't. "I was pretty close to the ground," Amy went on, "so I couldn't have been more than three. We were walking outside together, looking at the grass.

There was a little white moth on a piece of clover and suddenly a garter snake slid right up and ate it."

"My. How gruesome."

"I was fascinated. 'There you have it,' you said. 'The short happy life of Murray the moth.'"

Mrs. Adams smiled. "I think you made it up."

"I did *not*."

"I mean, your memory made it up."

"What's the first thing you remember, Gran? Unless it hurts to talk."

"Snow. Coming down outside my window. And then a cardinal flying by — red against white." She drifted into a doze again. Coming to sometime later, she pressed Amy's hand. "How's Kevin?"

"Finito."

"Phooey," Mrs. Adams said. It troubled her that Amy had never had a relationship of any real length.

Then it seemed that Amy dissolved and the doctor hovered over her, the hand he'd fastened to her wrist like ice against her fiery skin. "I just don't know," he said under his breath.

She fell asleep again, although it wasn't sleep exactly. She was aware of the room, and could hear all the voices—Amy's and the nurse's—but when she opened her eyes, she only saw through a kind of mist. There was a small rasping sound coming from her mouth. How rude, she thought.

Amy appeared beside her, an impressionist landscape—her face like the sun, her blue sweater a summer sky. "Pretty," Mrs. Adams said.

"You're my best friend, Gran," Amy whispered.

"Honored," Mrs. Adams said.

"What can I do to help you?" Amy asked. Her voice grew small. "Help you do this."

"Stay … if you can stand it."

"I'll do whatever you want me to."

"Don't be frightened."

There was a long pause. "Okay," Amy said finally. And then, "Are you?"

"Not so much. Curious ...." And then she was off again, halfway between here and there.

The next morning it began to rain, sighing in waves against the window. Mrs. Adams could hear it beyond the labored creak of her own breathing, each breath seeming to cost her all the strength she had left, until somehow she managed to summon the effort for one more, and then another. Speech was beyond her now. She sensed that Amy was there beside her. Others came and went as well, causing the room to vibrate softly with their movements.

Time took on the fluidity of a dream. She imagined she saw Stella and Amy sitting side by side on a picnic bench swinging their legs. In dream logic, they were contemporaries, though, rather than mother and daughter. Stella's bare knees were grimy as they'd always been in the summertime, and she jabbed at Amy's polka-dot shirt with her index finger the way Mrs. Adams' older cousin used to do to her. "Polka dots are for poking," he would say. It had always made Mrs. Adams frantic, but in the dream Amy just laughed.

"Can you hear me, Gran?" Amy was saying.

Mrs. Adams tried vainly to summon up the strength to answer. She felt sorry, hearing the sadness in Amy's voice. She couldn't stand for Amy to be sad. Even when she'd been a baby, crying as all babies cry, it had been unbearable.

Recently, Mrs. Adams had come to confuse Amy's birth with the lost baby, her own little boy who had died at one month because his underdeveloped lungs had become infected. Now that child, Jed, came into focus so clearly—his dark hair, pale skin, his lips round and pouty, the dimple on the left side of his mouth just like his older sister.

They'll tell you that it's just gas, but Jed was one of those babies who smile practically from the moment they're born. Mrs. Adams was forty, and for a long time she had blamed herself, among all kinds of other failures, for being too old to conceive a healthy child. She had been toppled by the depth of her grief. How was it possible to be nearly ruined by the loss of someone you'd only known a month? Nor did it end, not ever. It got easier, of course, but even now, not a year passed that she didn't remember the anniversaries, both birth and death. Feeling Amy's hand covering her own now, she recalled Jed's tiny fist grasping her index finger.

Midmorning, there was a disturbance at the outer door. She could hear male voices, busy with a masculine project of some kind.

She turned her head to Amy.

"It's the hospital bed," Amy said apologetically. "They're bringing it in."

Mrs. Adams lay still and listened to the invasion. She tried to lift her free hand but it lay helpless beside her. She concentrated. Perhaps if she relinquished the effort it cost her to take a breath, she'd have enough strength left to do this one last thing. She focused on her hand, willing it to rise to her face. Yes, it was working. She found the plastic tubing and pulled it from her nose.

"Oh, Gran," Amy said.

There were no words any more, but she could still look into Amy's face and tell her with her eyes. Amy gazed back at her, and Mrs. Adams saw that she understood.

After a while, the rattling sound of the hospital bed ceased. The voices were stilled. She heard weeping. It sounded like rain sweeping the surface of the ocean. Nothing hurt her any more. She closed her eyes and was lifted into the dark on a buoyant swell of gratitude.

NIGHT OF THE ANIMALS

Amy: 1980

The thing was, she didn't even *like* Theo. That was what was so remarkable. The first time she met him, she was sitting on the front steps of the town library after trying for an hour to research her history paper topic. She couldn't keep her mind on it, and after aimlessly flipping pages and doodling, had simply given up. A light snow was beginning to fall, freakish but not unheard of in April. She didn't bother to pull up the hood of her sweatshirt, just sat there with her rear end practically frozen to the concrete, trying to find a metaphor for how she was feeling: like the shell of a hermit crab, maybe, whose occupant had moved out. She could envision the "VACANCY" sign hanging off her, her eyes just empty holes you could look into, nothing inside.

Someone flipped her hood over her hair. She looked up to see an unfamiliar boy grinning down at her. "Guess what," he said. "It's snowing."

"I suppose that's because upstate New York still thinks it's winter."

He brushed the snow off a spot beside her and sat down. "Mind if I join you?"

Amy shrugged. She didn't care one way or the other. Although he was extremely good-looking, with clear blue eyes and dark hair falling across his forehead.

"I'm Theo," he said. "I've been waiting all week for a chance to meet you. It's the first day you haven't been surrounded by half a dozen girls."

It was true; ever since her parents separated, her friends

had been sticking to her like nettles. She knew she should be appreciative, but mostly she just wanted to be left alone. And now here was this person breathing her air. He did have a dazzling smile.

"You must have a really good dentist," she remarked.

He laughed. "Three years of braces. Amy, right?" He held out his hand. "Pleased to meet you." She didn't bother to ask how he knew her name.

On their first date, he took her to a bar. Amy could easily pass for twenty-one. Theo had brought along a fake ID that he'd had made up for her just in case — a very convincing driver's license that said she was from Topeka, Kansas. The photo was Marcia's, that slut, a close enough likeness if you didn't stare at it too long. Besides, it was so dark in there you could hardly see anything anyway.

It turned out that Theo was finishing up his sophomore year at the state college, which made him around twenty, Amy thought, five years older than she was, which didn't faze her especially. Older guys always seemed to like her. Even the father of one of the kids she babysat for had grabbed her thigh once in the car during the drive home.

"I'm a sophomore, too," she said. Thank God, she thought. They had tried to move her ahead two years ago. Her mother had been ecstatic, but Amy didn't want to leave the friends she'd been in class with since kindergarten. "What are you researching at the library?" she asked.

"Term paper on Dostoevsky. I found a great essay on *The Idiot*. It was even the exact right length."

Amy was surprised not to find herself more repelled by this. Since her decision to become a writer, she had developed fastidious habits of accreditation—the ownership of ideas was, to her, sacrosanct. She disapproved of Theo's casual larceny all right; she just couldn't work up a lather over it.

"What's your drink?" Theo asked her.

"I can't," Amy told him.

"Oh, come on. At least have a brew."

She explained about the hives.

"Well, then, I've got something just as good," Theo said, took a screw-top bottle out of his pocket and shook a capsule into his hand.

Amy hesitated.

"Honey, you are all twisted up in *knots*," Theo told her. "You need something to get you through the rough patch."

Gazing into his guileless eyes, she realized that she had no life. She was a husk, a milkweed pod, no heft to her at all any more.

"I'll make sure you're okay," he said.

And so she took the capsule from his palm and swallowed it dry. Pretty soon, she felt herself growing pleasantly warm, as if she were a hot water bottle being filled up. No more cold, no more emptiness. She smiled at Theo, at everyone in the bar. She smiled at the world.

"You're a magician," she said to Theo.

"Not really," he said, grinning. "I just wanted to see you happy."

He didn't sleep with her the first night. Not that she wasn't willing. Amy had never been so attracted to anyone in her life. After she swallowed the capsule, she found she could look straight through Theo's clothing, could see the long smooth muscles of his arms, the curve of his shoulders. She needed to have physical contact with him and kept her fingers on some part of him at all times. He seemed aglow to her, surrounded by pale light. He was a gift. And finally, after what seemed months to Amy, though it was actually only two weeks, he made love to her in the small apartment he rented off campus.

"I'm not a virgin," she said. She had matured early, years before her friends, but she had kept quiet about it. Not that she was ashamed; she simply guessed that they wouldn't understand.

Theo had given her another sort of pill an hour ago, a small yellow one this time. Her skin began to feel like it was shimmering, all the tiny hairs along her arms prickly, and standing at attention. It seemed miraculous to her that simply by ingesting a tiny scrap of yellow, a person could go from feeling nothing to feeling *everything*. She couldn't wait for him to touch her.

"I don't care if you're not a virgin," Theo said. "You're my clean pretty girl. You could never be anything but clean."

She supposed it was the drugs, but tonight she was a vessel full of words, words that kept replenishing themselves as she talked, talked, talked. Theo seemed keenly interested in her family, as if she were describing some fascinating alien species.

At some point, though, she realized that she knew next to nothing about him. She noticed the pale welts across his back and traced them with her fingers. "Did you have surgery?" she asked.

He just shook his head with a smile and climbed out of bed. When she questioned why he had left home when he was sixteen, he said, "Let's just say I was safer out of there." He hadn't been in touch with his parents for more than a year, a fact that floored Amy. She could barely imagine a week without contact with her own.

After that night, Amy spent all of her time with Theo or else plotting ways to meet him. She began to lose weight. Food didn't interest her, and it was hard to sleep because the drugs kept her pretty wired. She managed to skip out of school early most days by telling the principal that she was still recovering from mononucleosis and needed extra rest, her pallor lending the story credibility. She had an outstanding academic record and was president of her class. As Miss Solid Citizen, who would have doubted her?

The drugs were fantastic. And Theo was the best drug of all.

As the weeks passed, Tuesday nights became even more of a problem. Part of her parents' separation agreement stipulated that her father was to see her every Tuesday. Amy wondered who dreaded it the most. She was supposed to spend one weekend a month with him as well, though to Amy's relief, he hadn't yet called upon her to fulfill that one.

Once upon a time, Amy and her father had been close. He had liked poetry and would write her little rhymes in doggerel.

By the time she was ten, Amy was pretty deft at it as well. When she went to sleepaway camp one summer, she wrote poems to him about her friends and the horrible food. He would send back silly limericks about the family cat, poems she kept safe in a special black lacquer box.

Amy had also spent one of the happiest days of her childhood with him. Having decided that he was going to establish a commuter airline, he got himself a pilot's license and took Amy up with him. They didn't tell her mother ahead of time, but radioed her when they were already in the air, thinking it would be a delightful surprise. Stella didn't speak to Simon for a week, but it was worth it. Amy had the most glorious day. "Let's go to Cape Cod for lunch," her father said as they soared up over the treetops and into a summer sky. Cape Cod may as well have been the moon. They took a taxi from the little airport near Chatham to a clam shack and gorged themselves on steamers and lobster rolls. It could bring tears to her eyes when she thought about it now.

"Do you mind going to the mall for a bite?" Simon asked. "I need to pick up a couple of things."

"Fine," Amy said.

Most of the traffic as they drove east along Route Five was farm related: tractors, slow-moving trucks loaded with hay or corn to feed the dairy cows. Soon enough, the heavy vehicles would all turn off and disappear up the little ribbons of back roads that led home. Amy kept the window open so she could smell the fresh, green air. Neither she nor her father spoke. It used to be fun to ride with him. He'd had so many questions about her, as if she were the most interesting person he'd ever met. Not the standard stuff like her mother would ask—"How did your math test go?"—but "What does it feel like inside your head just before you fall asleep?" or, "If you could be one person for a day, who would it be?" All that now seemed like an awfully long time ago.

"Things going okay at school?" Simon asked finally, dutifully, his speech lapsing into the rhythm of his youthful tongue. Half British and when he was tired or less than comfortable, he started to sound like he was broadcasting over the BBC.

"Yeah," Amy answered. In the old days, before he'd turned into a non-person, he would have asked something like, "Which of your teachers has the best sense of humor?" or, "What was the worst thing they served in the cafeteria today?"

I used to like you, Amy thought. *I used to love you.* She knew for sure she used to call him "Daddy." Now she didn't call him anything. For so long now he had been more like a silent ghost in the house than a father. First he'd retreated into his tiny office where he stayed all day, often in his pajamas, to "work" on the computer, though everybody knew he was watching daytime television and tugging at his cheek with his fingers as if he were trying to peel his face off. Amy tried to talk to him. Tried and tried and tried again. He had simply looked at her as if she were something unfamiliar that had somehow strayed into his vision, like an eye floater. The poet was gone, and so was the pilot. The English didn't believe in therapy, Stella told her. Apparently they didn't believe in antidepressants, either, and one night he just packed up and left.

It got easier once they were inside the mall in Utica. There was the fast-food restaurant to choose—the trays to pick up, the food to order, the table to find, none of which required conversation. Amy sat across from her father in the busy food court and shot him a look from under her sun-bleached eyebrows as he twirled miserably at his spaghetti. He had buttoned his shirt wrong, a sure sign of a man who lived alone. The sudden pain in Amy's heart migrated to her throat and lodged there. She set her fork down.

"How's the new apartment?" she asked, giving up on dinner.

He lifted the corners of his mouth at her. "I haven't opened the cartons yet."

"Would you like me to come over and help?" It just slipped out.

"Oh, that's all right," he said. "I'll get around to it eventually."

· · ·

He dropped her off at eight. It was still almost light outside. Amy knew she should hunker down and start studying for her finals, but all she could think of was how to meet up with Theo. She reminded herself that she still had a chance to remain at the top of her class. Even with Theo. Even with the drugs. She tried to tell herself that she'd see Theo tomorrow. Maybe it wasn't such a long time to wait. He said he'd take her bowling. The idea appealed to her. Maybe she could make it through an entire evening without drugs.

On the way upstairs she was stopped in her tracks by an unearthly sound emanating from her mother's bedroom, a chilling wail that crawled up Amy's back and across her scalp, leaving a trail of goose bumps.

"Mom!" she cried out. "Mom!" She bolted the rest of the way up, nearly tripping on the top step in her haste. She half expected to intercept an intruder at the bedroom door, a serial killer who had left her mother lying fatally wounded in a pool of blood. The howling continued unabated as Amy catapulted into the room.

Stella was lying on the bed in the fetal position, clutching a pillow and splitting the air with her cries. The room felt damp and close, as if misery had sucked the oxygen out of it.

Amy sat down beside her mother and touched her shoulder. "Mom. Stop. You've got to stop."

The sound halted mid-scream as if someone had clicked the off button. She lay rigid and still.

"What's the matter, Mom? What can I do?" Amy asked. She stroked Stella's shoulder.

"Go away," Stella said.

"What?"

"Leave me alone."

Amy's hand fell to the bed and lay there, stunned, like a bird that had just slammed into a plate glass window. Stella rolled away from Amy and put the pillow over her head. Amy stood up. The room felt unsteady as if the floor were tilting. She grabbed the bureau to steady herself. Then she went to the telephone and called Theo.

* * *

Amy was the best-looking girl Theo had ever dated. Oh sure, her nose was a little asymmetrical and her front teeth overlapped just a bit, but as far as he was concerned these flaws only made her more adorable. Having a beautiful babe around had never posed a problem for him. *Most likely to succeed … with women*—this is what it said in his yearbook, right there below his photo. The guys gave him grief about Amy, called him a cradle snatcher. But Theo knew that they were just envious.

Theo loved nights like this, especially in his old MG, when he could put the top down and blaze through the summer night like a shooting star. He had some great shit on him, too, and looked forward to turning Amy on. She'd always looked so sad before, even surrounded by that pack of friends, but the drugs, they'd made her happy right from the start. That smile of hers could melt a glacier. Amy had sounded pretty hysterical over the phone just now, but he could take care of that in no time. He loved that, loved being the instrument of her joy. Watching the shadows leave her face, listening to her laughter, it was better than any pharmaceutical.

Maybe it was a little weird, given the drugs and the sex, but Amy had a purity about her. Theo had noticed that from the beginning, the way she sat in the library turning a strand of shiny blonde hair around her finger while she read. She always smelled so clean, like fresh air, like something that lived in a garden. He liked having that in his life for a change, so different from anything he'd known growing up. You never knew what kind of lowlife would stagger out of his mother's bedroom in the morning. When he left four years ago, it was tough coming up with money for an apartment and gas for the car, but the drug business soon took care of that and then some. He knew it wasn't forever. One of these days he'd need to get started on a real career. But in the meantime, he was having the best time of his life. So what if Amy was young? Down the road, a difference of five years? It wouldn't mean squat. The fact that he was actually thinking about a future with her kind of amazed him. This was a whole new thing.

. . .

Rather than dropping her off a block from the house as he normally did, Theo had insisted on taking her all the way home. "It's 2:00 a.m.," he said. "The last thing I want is to set your old lady off into mother bear mode."

"Not likely," Amy had answered. "Not even with a nuclear device."

He pulled up to the curb and leaned in to kiss her good night.

"I didn't know I could *ever* feel this good," Amy said.

Surely Theo's heart was visible through his shirt, he thought, pulsing with a warm and golden light. Gone, the inner fireball of anger ordinarily afflicting him, like a serious case of indigestion. Incredible. He was *always* angry.

He laid his hand against Amy's cheek. "Your eyes are like disco balls," he said. "Better not stare at anybody for a few hours." He gave her a gentle push and watched as she walked slowly away from the car. She kept stopping to look up at the trees with that big smile on her face. God knew what she was seeing. She must have a real party going on in her head.

It was too beautiful to go inside. Amy sat down on the front steps of the house and felt the breeze ripple like silk against her bare arms. She reached out, convinced she could catch the soft fabric in her hands, but it eluded her. She gazed up into the branches of the weeping willow. Its slender leaves were swaying in a rhythmic waltz. And just beyond, the stars throbbed along with the night music. She loved it all so much. She was overflowing with summer, with song, with joy. Why would she ever want to sleep again?

There was a soft sound beside her, like the clearing of a throat. She turned and saw a cricket sitting on the step beside her. She stared at it for a moment.

"What?" the cricket said.

"Did you say something?" Amy asked.

"I believe I asked you first."

Amy let out a long breath. "I must be really stoned."

"You got that right," the cricket said.

Amy sat very still. Moths beat against the front hall window where the light escaped from the house, making small sounds of frustration. Their voices, like the delicate patter of spring raindrops, were barely audible, but by listening carefully, she could make out a few phrases.

"What's the issue here?"

"Could we be doing something wrong?"

"I'm getting a migraine."

"Cool," Amy said. "I think I'm getting the hang of this." All at once, she realized that the cicadas were having some sort of contest. "I'm louder than you!" one shouted. "No, *meeeeeeee!*" came the reply from the far end of the lawn. "Me! Me! Me!" hollered another from across the street. So that was what it was all about, Amy thought. No wonder they make such a racket. When she turned her head, the darkness rained sequins that settled on the ground beside her feet and slowly faded.

"Here comes trouble," the cricket said. It hopped off the step and crawled under the porch.

The neighbor's old dog was sauntering up the sidewalk, his tail wagging slowly like a tired flag.

"Hey, Bob!" Amy exclaimed, delighted. He was half black Lab, half poodle, with his glossy coat parted down the middle of his back. One eye was blind and cloudy but the other, a lustrous brown, studied her carefully. Amy held her breath, hoping he'd have something to say.

"Looking a little the worse for wear," Bob said. His voice was deep and roughened by age. He sat down on the pavement and scratched himself with his back leg.

"Is that why this is happening?" Amy asked. "Because I'm wrecked out of my mind?"

"Absolutely," said Bob. Amy watched his mouth closely. It hadn't moved, and yet she could hear him so clearly.

"But it feels incredibly *real*."

"You're stoned but you're not crazy," Bob said.

"If anything, I feel less crazy now than I do when I'm sober."

"Well, then, that's a serious problem," Bob said.

"It's the emptiness," Amy said. "I can take anything but that. It's like being a jack-o'-lantern. Hollow."

"What about reading? As I recall, that used to fill you up."

From the time she was eight, Amy had been gobbling up books like snack food. By the time she was ten, she was reading Dickens and Tolkien. She liked being transported to a place where she could settle in and stay for a while. She liked detail, the more the better. She wanted to be able to visualize the color of the characters' hair, the shape of their hands, even the buttons on their clothes.

"You have to read if you're going to be a writer," Bob went on.

"I just can't seem to get into a book now," Amy said. "I don't write any more either. Not even in my journal. All I can ever think about is my boyfriend. He's changed my life completely."

"I met him, remember?"

"Right, I forgot," Amy said. "Out by your yard the other night. What did you think of him?"

"To tell the truth, he gave off a faint scent of misogyny." Bob circled around a couple of times and lay down at her feet.

"Wow, you don't hold back, do you?"

"I'm not telling you anything you don't know, am I? Scratch my shoulder, will you?"

Amy obliged. "Theo came along at just the right time," she said. "Like an angel."

"As you well know, he stole electronics from the company where he had a summer job," Bob said. "And now he makes his money selling drugs. Some angel."

"Okay, I know all that, but just the same I can't imagine my life without him. I felt *dead*. Even feeling *bad* is better than feeling *dead*."

Bob got up with a sigh and laid his muzzle on Amy's lap. "You remember how I got this blind eye?" he asked. "You were there. You saved my life."

"The hit and run?"

"Precisely. I was lying there more dead than alive and you called the taxi. That driver took one look at me and started to take off, but you hung onto the door and bullied him into taking us to the vet. You stayed with me while they set my leg." His voice was growing dim. Amy had to concentrate hard to hear him. She ran her fingers over his silky ears.

"Look, honey," he said. Amy bent her head down close. "I used to love chasing cars. Couldn't get enough. I was a total thrill junkie. I'd hide behind the Robertsons' azaleas and run out when I saw one coming. Got away with it for years until that day. And, see, this is just what you're doing. Chasing cars. You've gotta find another way or …"

She couldn't hear the last part. "What did you say? Or what?"

"… Road hash. You'll wind up as road hash." He lifted his head off her thigh and walked down the sidewalk, limping slightly, his nails clicking against the cement.

Amy woke up in a heap beside the front steps. It was just getting light and the birds had set up an awful squawking. No conversations now, just horrible ear-splitting shrieks that made her head throb. She had a sour taste in her mouth, every part of her body stiff and aching, as if she'd been thrashed with a tree limb. Worse than the physical pain, though, was the bleakness that filled her like a sackful of darkness. She wished she were lying off in the woods where nobody would find her for days. She could just stop breathing. That ought to be easy enough. Water began to seep out of the corners of her eyes. Oh, the pain, the pain. She thought about last night, about the dog. Road hash, that was what he had said.

She began to haul herself up the steps and watched the progress of her knees, focusing on her forward movement and trying not to think, just allowing raw impulse to propel her. When she reached the top, she crawled past the dry corpse of a moth and reached for the front doorknob to pull herself to her feet. Tears spilled down to dampen the neckband of her t-shirt.

The phone was all the way at the entrance to the kitchen, miles away. Slowly, slowly she crept towards it. Grabbing the receiver finally, she collapsed with her back to the wall. Theo'll have something for me, she thought, something to make me feel better. She began to dial, stopped after three numbers and let out a sob. The phone seemed to have a life of its own; somehow it wound up back in its cradle. Next she dialed again, different numbers this time.

"Hell-LOH-oh," the voice said, sleepy but characteristically welcoming.

"Gran," Amy whispered. And then she began to cry in earnest.

"Amy," Mrs. Adams said. "What's the matter?"

Amy couldn't stop crying.

"You have to get a grip on yourself and tell me what's happened," Mrs. Adams said. "Are you hurt? Were you in an accident?" Any trace of sleep was utterly gone from her voice.

"I'm a mess, Gran."

"I can hear that. Take some deep breaths. Do it now."

Amy did as she was told. It took a few tries, but finally she regained control of her sobs.

"Let me just put on the light," Mrs. Adams said. "There."

"Can I come and stay with you for a while?" Amy asked.

"Of course you can."

"Will you fix it with Mom?"

"Certainly. Why don't you put her on the phone?"

"No!" Amy almost shouted. "I mean, please don't make me talk to her. I just … can't." She felt herself beginning to cry again.

Mrs. Adams heard the tears threaten. "Amy, darling, do you want me to come and get you?"

Amy thought for a moment. It felt good to address something concrete. A journey. She imagined her grandmother showing up here to collect her, the collision with her mother. "No. I can do it. I'll get the early train and take a taxi from the station."

"Do you have enough money for all this?"

"I think so."

"Are you sure you're well enough to do this on your own?"

"I've done it a hundred times, Gran."

"Come along then. Let's get you on that early train."

. . .

The first thing Mrs. Adams did after she hung up the phone was to go into the bathroom and splash cold water on her face. The heat must have come on during the night, even though Mrs. Adams always turned the thermostat down to fifty on the first day of spring. Her nightgown clung to her skin. She was glad William couldn't see her in it. He would have thought it dowdy. She glanced at the twin beds side by side, his made up neatly, as always, ready for his return. It had been four years and she still caught herself waiting.

At eight o'clock, she phoned her daughter. Stella did not express her jealousy that Amy would turn to Mrs. Adams instead of her. Nor did Stella disclose her own desire to run home to mother right at that moment, given her current emotional state. Not that she ever would.

"I'll phone you as soon as she gets here," Mrs. Adams said calmly, and they hung up.

It was nearly noon by the time Amy showed up. Mrs. Adams had been watching for the taxi and went out to pay the driver when it pulled up out front. Amy hauled a suitcase and a backpack out of the trunk and set them on the sidewalk. She was taller than her grandmother by a couple of inches and stood looking down at her with tear-filled eyes. Mrs. Adams hid her shock at the dark blotches under them, the unwashed hair, the sallow complexion.

"I'm sorry, Gran," Amy said.

Mrs. Adams held out her arms. "The first thing we're going to do is feed you. You're skin and bones."

"Do you think it's possible to be addicted to a person?" Amy asked. She was sitting in the kitchen across the table from Mrs. Adams, who was plying her with pita bread and hummus. Amy didn't like baked goods or ice cream, so it took some imagination to fatten her up.

"I don't see why not," Mrs. Adams said. In fact, now that she thought about it, perhaps addiction was merely a more accurate term for being in love. "Tell me about this young man."

"Well, he's not what you'd call a *good* person, not that I even care. I've always been so high and mighty, like when my friends drink too much and get all sloppy? And here I'm doing sex and drugs with a guy who's for sure a dealer and maybe worse."

Mrs. Adams was struck by her own reaction to this confession. There was no struggle to disguise judgment, for she felt none, merely a knot of fear lodged behind her rib cage. How different it had been with Stella.

"I was feeling invisible, you know? And he, he just looked right at me from the first second, the way *you* do. I probably shouldn't, I know, but I just … trust him."

Mrs. Adams regarded her quietly.

"I know," Amy said. She gave her grandmother a wan smile, pushing her plate away. "I miss him so much I'd just as soon die if I can't see him again."

"Did you tell him you were leaving?"

Amy shook her head. "He would have talked me out of it. I would have stayed." She had changeable eyes, right now greener than they were blue, small oceans of sadness.

"Amy, darling," Mrs. Adams said, reaching her hand across the table to capture the slender fingers, "you are far too old for your age."

It must not have taken long for her to fall asleep. Mrs. Adams saw that the girl had simply sprawled out fully dressed with her backpack beside her. There was a little stretch of exposed flesh between the waistband of her jeans and her t-shirt. Mrs. Adams tiptoed over and carefully pulled it down. Amy didn't stir. Then she went downstairs and got out her phonebook.

Fritz Jenovyk had been nineteen when Mrs. Adams first met him. William had been away on a business trip, so she was alone when the police called at 2:00 a.m. It turned out that Fritz had stolen Mrs. Adams' car from the driveway and crashed it into a tree out on the West Hill Road. What she saw when she got to the police station was just a farm boy; he might as well have been balancing on the top of a split-rail fence. It was clear to her that this young man could fall either way. He was sorry and defiant, vulnerable and tough-talking, quick-witted but uneducated. Most of all he was desperate, with the longest eyelashes she had ever seen and large hands with nails bitten down to the quick.

Not only did Mrs. Adams refuse to press charges, but she met privately with him and gave him a loan from her "just in case" fund, the account that nobody knew about. More even than the money, Fritz needed a gesture, some expression of faith. He wound up working his way through college, as things turned out, and repaid Mrs. Adams every penny of the loan.

"Fritz?" Mrs. Adams said into the phone, keeping her voice low. "Are you going to be around over the next week or two? I may need you."

Amy spent the first two days with her head in the toilet bowl.

"Did I feed you something that didn't agree with you?" Mrs. Adams held a washcloth to Amy's head as they sat side by side on the bathroom floor, the cool, hard marble cruel against her sixty-nine-year-old bones.

"It's the drugs," Amy said. When she wasn't vomiting, she was either asleep or crying, sometimes both.

"Should I take you to the hospital?" Mrs. Adams asked her. "Or one of those places that helps get you off the drugs?"

Amy grasped Mrs. Adams' hand and held on tight. "Please don't send me away, Gran."

On the fourth day, just when Amy had begun to get a little color back in her cheeks, the event that Mrs. Adams had been dreading came to pass. He showed up at about four o'clock in the afternoon. Thankfully, Amy was napping upstairs and didn't hear him knock. The young man stood handsome and smiling in the doorway.

"Hi," he said, holding out his hand. "You Amy's grandmother?"

"You must be Theo," Mrs. Adams said, standing her ground, arms at her sides. With his shiny black hair and clear eyes, he was the epitome of wholesome youth.

"I really need to see her," he said. "Can I come in?"

"How did you know she was here?" Mrs. Adams asked.

"Oh, she talks about you. She says you're her best friend."

"Please wait on the porch," Mrs. Adams said, closing the screen door against him.

Her legs were wobbling as she went into the kitchen to pick up the telephone. Fritz had to be paged, but thankfully they were able to track him down.

"It's Lily Adams," she told him. "He's here. Can you come?"

Hanging up, she braced against the table, staring down at the tablecloth. It was sprinkled with a pattern of yellow and purple pansies that seemed at this moment absurd.

"Gran?"

She turned to see Amy in the doorway. "What's going on? I thought I heard talking."

"I'd like you to go back upstairs," Mrs. Adams said quietly.

Amy studied her. "Theo's here, isn't he?"

"I want you to let me handle this," Mrs. Adams said. "You're in no condition."

"He came for me," Amy said.

"Yes," Mrs. Adams said. She looked at the clock on the kitchen wall. The second hand clung stubbornly to each demarcation before finally lurching to the next.

A car pulled up out front. Amy and Mrs. Adams both moved to the window. Striding up the sidewalk was a hulking state trooper in full regalia. Amy clutched Mrs. Adams.

"What's going on?" she whispered.

But Mrs. Adams disengaged herself and opened the front door. "Fritz, thank you for coming over." Amy stepped out behind her. "Amy, this is Officer Jenovyk."

"Amy," Theo said from the porch, starting for her.

Fritz held out an arm. "Stay where you are, son."

"Oh, Theo," Amy said. "Gran, please. Just for a minute?"

"No, darling, I don't think it's wise."

"How about we take a walk to your vehicle," Fritz said to Theo.

"I need to speak to my girlfriend," Theo said.

Fritz clamped a hand on Theo's shoulder. "Let's take a walk," he said.

Halfway down the sidewalk, Theo turned back to look at Amy. He had the look of someone who has just collided with a brick wall. Fritz opened the door to the MG and deposited Theo inside. The trooper's large frame dwarfed the car as he leaned in to speak with Theo. Amy went out onto the porch and sat down on the steps with her face hidden on her arms. Mrs. Adams stood beside her, watching. Finally, Fritz stood up, slapped the trunk of Theo's car and backed away.

"That's it," they heard him say.

Theo started the car. He didn't look at Amy, just slid slowly off down the quiet street. Amy sat with her head on her knees, shaking convulsively. After Mrs. Adams said good-bye to Fritz she came to sit beside Amy.

"Oh Gran," Amy said. The hair around her face was damp with tears. "How am I ever supposed to be happy again?"

Mrs. Adams took her in her arms and rocked her gently. She couldn't get Theo's face out of her mind, the expression as he gazed at Amy with such intense need. "Yes, you'll be happy," she told Amy. "Then you won't be. Then you will again."

Amy was silent a moment. "Okay," she said finally. After a while, her sobs died away, and the two sat quietly, old and young, in the late afternoon.

IN HER BONES

Stella: 1955

The new boy didn't look like anyone Stella had ever seen before. He was only three years older than she was, which made him seventeen, but he carried himself like an adult. It was partly the English accent, she supposed, but he also had a certain poise, a watchful quality like he was taking it all in and carefully making up his mind. She couldn't imagine him grabbing hold of the vine over in Lars Woods and swinging himself out over the ravine like Eric or Fred.

"We'll have a guest at brunch today," Stella's mother had told her that Sunday before leaving for the country club. "His mother's an old friend of mine who lives in England."

"The pretty one who comes to visit sometimes?" Stella asked.

"Yes, and Simon's actually been here once or twice himself, but you must have been away at camp. Grace and I grew up together in Egypt."

"Oh, yeah. The story with the crabs."

Lily and Grace had spent a summer living in a luxurious tent community near Alexandria. Every evening as the sun went down, the fiddler crabs, hundreds of them, would march over the hard sand along the surf. Lily still remembered the sight with awe.

"There are some people who stay with you always," she told Stella. "It doesn't matter how often you see them."

"What's her son doing here now?" Stella asked. She was helping her mother fold the laundry that had just come off the line out back. Lily Adams was one of the few people left in town who passed up the dryer, at least during the warm months. Her husband teased her about it. They had plenty of household help, after all, but Lily liked the smell of sunshine and fresh air as she gathered the clean clothes into her arms.

"He's taking a summer course at the college. It's been a hard few years for him, so please be cordial."

This rankled. Of *course* Stella would be cordial. When was she ever rude? It was so irritating when her mother expected only the worst from her. "Why was it hard?" she asked.

"He lost his brother."

"Oh," Stella said. She buried her face in a bath towel. If anything ever happened to anyone she loved—her mother, say—she didn't think she could face another hour of the day. She felt Lily's hand on her head.

"Let's go get dressed, shall we? I intend to dazzle. How about you?"

Lily Adams didn't learn to drive until after Stella was born. Having grown up in a series of foreign cities with missionary parents who never considered an automobile license a priority for their daughter, she was uneasy behind the wheel and somewhat inept. Stella braced herself now, on their way to the country club, as their tires dug briefly into the shoulder on the right. She couldn't wait to get her learner's permit. She already knew how to drive the car up and down their driveway, but by now that had grown pretty tiresome.

It had puzzled some of their wealthy friends when William and Lily had opted to join the local club rather than the more exclusive one over in New Hartford. William's father, after all, and then William himself, had headed the prosperous furniture company that his grandfather had founded, the firm that employed most of the town. Furthermore, the local golf course had only nine holes and its tennis courts were weedy. Worst of all, there was a large dairy farm directly across Route 48. Sometimes, when the wind was right, the heady scent of cows floated directly onto the clubhouse patio. Still, Lily and William enjoyed the inclusiveness of the membership there that ranged from the mail clerk at Adams Manufacturing Limited to the mayor himself.

"With this kid around, I guess Dad won't be able to play tennis with me," Stella grumbled as they shuddered their way up the long bumpy road to the clubhouse. There was no point in even waiting for a response. Her mother didn't like to talk while she was driving for fear of losing her concentration. "I suppose we can do a round-robin," Stella murmured.

The new boy and Stella's father were already sitting at a table when Stella and Lily entered the dining room. Lily was effortlessly elegant, as always, in a pale coral sweater that flattered her fine skin and chestnut hair. Stella had yanked on her one skirt and a cotton blouse with pictures of buffaloes stenciled down the front. She had traded a friend for it, getting rid of a preppy pink shirt that annoyed her. Stella's concept of fashion had always been somewhat unorthodox. As a three-year-old, she insisted upon wearing her favorite pajamas to nursery school. She was a willful child, so Lily had simply sighed, deciding that this was not a battle worthy of engagement. As long as she was clean and warm, what did it matter?

William was deep into a conversation with the boy. Lily touched her husband's shoulder, and when he turned to her the expression on his handsome, weathered face changed as if someone had just told him he won the lottery. "Lily," he said. "Here's our Simon. Stella, this is Simon Vanderwall."

Stella had already extended her hand in the way she had of stretching out to greet the world. She sat across from Simon and gazed at him, looking into his face for tragedy and finding none.

"How was your golf lesson?" William asked.

"It's tomorrow after school," Stella said.

"Stella's a real natural," he explained to Simon. Stella ducked her head, embarrassed. Her father loved to find an excuse to bring up her athletic prowess. "But she doesn't much bother to practice."

Stella bet he remembered perfectly well when her lesson

was, and bet he just pretended he thought it was today so that he could brag to the new boy. She didn't even like golf. It was much too slow for her, all that standing around before you even got a chance to finally swing at the ball. She far preferred tennis.

"Simon, it must be a little strange for you here," Lily said. "You have so many attachments to America through your father, I know, but it can't feel much like home."

Stella watched the boy's face as he fastened his eyes on her mother, clearly moved by her sensitivity and grateful for it. Stella had seen the same phenomenon a hundred times. Her mother, she decided, saw directly into people's hearts and then would choose the perfect words to offer comfort. The only exception was Stella, who seemed to baffle everyone, including her mother and certainly herself.

"I used to spend summers at my grandparents' in Nebraska," Simon said, "but, yes, mostly it seems like home is somewhere in the middle of the Atlantic."

"I hope you'll come to us often while you're here," Lily said, and winked at him. "I have stories to tell you about your mother."

As usual, people began to stop by at their table: the Comptons with their two children, one as nasty as the other was adorable; the doctor, a widower, who had delivered Stella; the company's head of sales, whose ruddy complexion hinted at high blood pressure. It was always like this, people paying their respects to the royal family. Stella thought she might scream. She folded and refolded her napkin. There was something forced about her father's congeniality today, she thought, glancing at the empty martini glass on the table in front of him. At lunch? Sure, there were always cocktails before dinner, and maybe a glass or two of wine, but she had never seen him drink at this hour.

"What are you taking at the college?" she asked Simon.

He turned his gray eyes on her and she felt a funny sensation in her stomach, like a guitar string bring plucked. "Twentieth century American lit and Shakespeare's comedies," he answered.

"You came all the way over here for Shakespeare?" Stella asked.

"Sure," he answered. "Why, don't you like him?"

"Oh, I'm too young for that stuff," she said. "And probably too dumb." She could have stabbed herself with the salad fork. She really liked the way he wore his hair, shaggy and long enough to brush the collar of his shirt.

"I really doubt that," Simon said and gave her a smile. Oh, there it was, she saw now, the sadness. That smile was sincere, all right, but filtered through a broken heart. She felt like reaching across the table and taking his hand. Out of the corner of her eye, she noticed that her father had somehow procured another martini and had swallowed most of it. She knew he was angry at her grandfather, as usual, for interfering at the company. For several weeks, he'd been blowing up over stupid things. Just the other day, he broke another tennis racquet after a bad shot and yelled at her mother because his pants had come back from the cleaners with the crease in the wrong place. Stella wanted to slug him when he hurt her mother.

They made their trips to the buffet table, and as Stella, Lily and Simon chatted, William continued to drink. He was conversing plenty, just not with *them*, craning his neck over to the next table instead.

"You're not addressing the ball properly!" he lectured the school superintendent. "I was watching you just this morning! You know what'll help? Square dancing! I'm not kidding!"

Stella felt a flush creep up her neck and flood her cheeks. Her father was practically shouting. People were turning to look at him.

"Waiter!" he called, and plucked at the sleeve of a passing busboy. "Martini. Two olives."

Lily returned to the table and touched his arm. "Don't you think you've had enough, William?" she asked.

He barely broke stride. "There's a square dance at the Legion on Monday nights!"

Please, God, Stella thought. Make him stop shouting. Lily laid her hand on his. He shook it off and glared at her. "Don't manage me, Lily," he snapped, and turned back to the superintendent.

"Check out that dance!" William bellowed. "Can't tell

you how it works, but there's something about balance. And it wouldn't hurt to lose some weight!"

The man and his wife bobbed their heads with the stunned look of trapped animals when the cage door clangs shut. Stella wadded her napkin into a tortured ball on her lap. He was drunk. Her father was drunk. She'd only seen one person inebriated in her life, that horrible Mrs. Brickles who would get out on the dance floor by herself and writhe around like a stripper and try to sing with the band even though she could never remember the words. How could Stella go back to school and face the superintendent in the hallway? Stella looked at her mother. Do something, she thought. Make him stop. Make him sober. Make him go away. But Lily, her face ashen, could only stare at William like everyone else.

"I propose a toast to the new regime!" William shouted, staggering to his feet. "To International Furnishers, I-N-C, cretins and infidels, long may they reign!" He drained his glass, then hurled it to the floor where it shattered loudly. His knees buckled as he attempted to sit. Stella saw what was coming. She put her hands to her head and whispered, "No ...."

The chair skidded out from under William as he crashed to the floor. His legs flailed in the air a moment, cartoonlike, revealing his socks and several inches of bare leg. And then it was over. There was immediate and profound silence, as if one of those remote controls had suddenly clicked on mute. Finally, after what seemed an eternity to Stella, the occupants of the nearby tables went to help Lily lift her father up. Stella fled.

She locked herself in the last stall of the ladies' room and wept with great heaving sobs. She felt, when she cried like this, as if she were on the ocean in a tempest, forty-foot waves sweeping her up where she hung suspended, gasping, only to be flung down again into the trough below. After a while, there was a knock on the door. Stella saw Lily Adams' shoes outside the stall. They were spectator pumps, not a scuff mark on them, lined up side by side, as if her mother were standing at attention.

"Stella," Lily commanded. "Open the door."

"I wish he would *die*!" Stella shot back even as the wave

swept her up. She took a deep shuddering breath, then howled as she plummeted down again. "I hate him! I hate him to *death*!"

"Open the door this instant," Lily said. "Don't force me to fetch Mr. Davis to get you out."

The door slowly swung open, but Stella remained inside, slumped forward on the lid of the toilet seat, still sobbing.

Lily took her by the shoulders. "You have to get control of yourself. Now calm down, Stella. *Right* now."

"You just sat there watching him get drunk," Stella said, her words punctuated by gulps. "Everyone saw him fall on his butt. And that new boy …" She buried her face in her hands.

"I don't know how to talk to you when you're like this," Lily said. "It can't be good for you, these hysterics."

Stella had been hearing this all her life. Her mother never shouted, hardly ever raised her voice. "Don't you have *any* feelings, Mama? Didn't you feel humiliated right there in front of everybody? In front of Simon?"

Lily's eyes closed, and for just a moment a deep line appeared between her brows. Now I've hurt her, Stella thought. I'm horrible. A horrible daughter with a horrible father. She leapt up and pushed her way past Lily, felt the futile brush of her mother's fingers on her arm and then she was out of there, dashing down the hallway with its portraits of local golf champions and its subtle smell of carpet mold and Sunday cooking.

By the front door stood a figure silhouetted against the sunshine with his back to her, hands in pockets. Stella would have to get past him and dreaded speaking to anyone. Having heard her approach, the figure turned around. It was Simon Vanderwall.

"Oh, no!" Stella cried out.

She tried to slip around him, but he grabbed her arm. She looked at him with tears pouring down her cheeks. His face floated in front of her. It seemed a portrait of grief. He had lost his brother, she remembered.

As for her little Sunday brunch tragedy? Her father had made a fool of himself, that was all. Nobody had died. She was so ashamed. "Aren't you going to tell me it's no big deal?" she asked Simon.

"No."

"I don't know what to do," Stella said. She couldn't help it. She was still on the ocean, at the mercy of the storm.

"Is there anywhere you can go?" Simon asked. He had kept his hand wrapped around her upper arm.

Those fingers felt good. "Yes," she said finally. "I do have a place."

"Would you like me to go with you?"

She looked out across the parking lot where rows of cars baked in the sun, their colors reflecting painfully into her swollen eyes. "Okay," she said. "If you can stand me."

Parson's Creek, a half-mile hike from the country club, divided two counties of rural upstate New York that rose gently northward from the wide valley along the Mohawk River. Beginning in what was little more than a large puddle atop a glacial ridge, the stream gathered volume as it flowed downhill joined by other runoff, cascading over sheer rock and meandering through cow pastures. The gulch, as it was known, was a wooded stretch where the creek had carved through sediment and clay, a sanctuary with pristine water eddying between flat sun-warmed rocks. There had been an effort two years ago to buy up some land creekside for development, put to rest only when it was determined that annual spring floods would render the plan impractical. Stella was so relieved. She was profoundly attached to the countryside around Indian Wells, and felt particularly proprietary about the gulch.

During the trek across the golf course, along the fence of a cow pasture and into a patch of trees, Stella said nothing. When they reached the gulch she sat down cross-legged on a rock.

Simon rolled up his pant legs, removed his shoes and socks, and sat beside her, dangling his feet in the water. Later, he would remember the icy cold and the way she had looked beside him. She had a pouty upper lip that showed a bit of her teeth. Probably, she had sucked her thumb as a little girl.

He hoped she would never get braces and spoil the effect. He could not remember ever meeting anyone whose emotions lay so close to the surface, as if her skin were simply a transparent film behind which the drama of her life played out for all to see. She had taken such delight in her food at the table, he noticed, really tasting each forkful, unlike Simon, who ate because he had to. As for her father, she had looked at him at one point with something close to adoration and at the next with loathing.

"I'm sorry about the crying," she said. "I get sort of lost."

"Are you all right now?"

"Long as I don't think about him."

"Then don't," he said.

"If only it were that easy." She made a gulping noise as she tried to wrestle back a new round of tears. "He's crazy sometimes, mangles his tennis racquet, yells at other drivers on the road …" She gazed at Simon helplessly as her weeping resumed and began gathering momentum. "I'm sorry," she gasped. "I'm so sorry …"

He reached over to remove Stella's sandals and set her feet one by one into the water. It felt perfectly natural, that he should handle her like that.

"There's something wrong with me," she said, the tears lessening a bit from the shock of the ice cold water. "It's like I'm crying because I'm crying."

"It's what you do, that's all," Simon said. "Maybe if you stop worrying about it so much, you'll feel calmer."

This was a new thought. It sat in her brain like a smooth round stone. She felt herself grow quieter. The cold water washing over her toes helped as well.

"My mother says my emotions are 'untidy,'" she said finally.

"She must have been upset as well."

"Oh, she'll just go read on her bed with the door closed. That's what *she* does when he's impossible."

"If the door's closed, how do you know she's reading?"

"Well, she's not crying like I do, that's for sure."

"But how do you know for sure?"

"Because I've listened at the door." She cupped some water

and splashed it over her face, cooling her flushed skin. "I wish there was something I could do to keep it from happening ever again."

"Maybe there is," he said. "It's the past you can never change."

They sat in silence for a moment, the water babbling rhythmically as it spilled around their feet.

"You mean about your brother," Stella said.

He didn't respond.

"I'm sorry," Stella said. Her mother never would have mentioned it. She always knew when to keep her mouth shut.

"That's all right. I'm glad you know about it."

Stella decided to keep quiet and wait. She concentrated on the water.

"He was my twin," Simon said after a moment.

"How terrible," Stella said.

"It was. It is. We used to dream about the same things on the same night." His eyes widened in surprise at his own admission.

Stella imagined the two of them comparing notes in the morning. "That seems like some crazy kind of sorcery," she said.

"It seemed normal to us, though." He was quiet, remembering. "Anyway, you can't change what's happened. It's like trying to change the sun or the stars. The past is there already. It's just … there."

Stella wanted to hug him in the worst way. Instead, she covered his hand with hers for a moment and waited for him to continue. It was what her mother would have done, she was certain, neither press him nor jump in with her own thoughts. She decided that she liked herself more when she was sitting beside this boy. She glanced at his legs, bare below the knee. The shape of them under that haze of blond hair seemed elegant to her.

"It's beautiful here," Simon said finally. "Not at all what I would have thought of New York."

Stella kicked her feet in the water, cheered and grateful that he would appreciate this special place.

"Who are the Indians in Indian Wells?" he asked.

"The Oneidas—part of the Iroquois nation. They were the only tribe that supported the colonists during the revolution. They fought side by side in really bloody battles up here, and all they got from the government was a piece of cloth. Plus being kicked off their land."

Simon smiled at her passion. This girl didn't feel halfway about anything.

"What about Parson's Creek? Why Parson's?"

"I have no idea," Stella said.

Simon laughed.

"My mother brought me to this place," Stella said. "Starting when I was really little. We made things from the clay. Of course, her pots and dishes were always lopsided, like her cakes. She's a horrible baker. Everything looks like somebody sat down on one half."

Simon smiled at her. He would have liked to reach over and brush the tears from her cheeks, but they had pretty much dried by now.

"What clay?" he said. "Show me."

Stella got up and waded to the bank. She dug into the earth, discarding the pebbles until she'd collected a lump of buff-colored clay. Simon held out his hand as she returned to him with it.

"See how easy it is to shape?" Stella said. "Here. Make an ashtray. That's the easiest."

She watched his hair fall across his forehead as he bent to the task, gratified that she'd distracted him from the pain she saw in his face when he spoke about his brother. "I liked making ballerinas," she said after a while. "Only I could never keep their arms and legs from breaking off. That's a really nice ashtray, you know, for your first try. Press a little indentation in the rim for the cigarette to rest on, like so. And we'll let it dry in the sun. Tomorrow it'll be perfect." Tomorrow, she thought, I will see him.

He laughed, a lovely deep chortle. "It's for you," he said. "In case you take up smoking cigars."

She settled in beside him again. "What do you do," she

asked. "For fun, I mean?"

"Read."

"Read what?"

"Poetry and fiction mostly. I like stories with a lot of characters."

"I get bored with reading."

"I don't think I've ever been bored in my life."

"Well, what if you had to just sit here? Not do anything for, say, ten minutes?"

He thought it over. "Look at that," he said, pointing down at their feet.

"What? Our feet?"

"Look at the way the water flows over our toes," he said. "The way the sun and the shadows splinter the light. It's like jewels. Like a stained glass window. I could stare at that for hours." He smiled again. "Although eventually, I suppose, our feet would freeze."

Tears stung her eyes, but these were different, so different from the ones before. She couldn't explain it, but his words and his presence flooded her with something potent and physical. Her throat constricted, her skin tingled, her breath fluttered. She felt *aware,* as if more alive than ever before, of gratitude, of appreciation, for this moment so profound that she could feel her very bones absorbing the sounds of the water, the dappled light, the smell of damp earth, the soft accent of Simon's voice, the two pairs of feet side by side.

"Don't go back to London," she said.

"Well, I won't, not for a while," he said.

"No, I mean ever. Just don't ever go back. You have to stay here forever."

With me, she thought. With me forever.

ELEVEN MINUTES

Simon: 1953

Listening to Professor Boyd read *Othello* was brain food for Simon. That's what London meant—lit class, the museums, and now that he was older, an occasional concert or play. All that stimulation made him happy enough, but even so, some part of him was always loose in the wild country of Devonshire where he and his brother had spent their summers.

So when their parents decided that it would be prudent, given Jeremy's proclivity for misconduct at the rigid St. Stephen's School, to move the boys to the country house permanently, Simon's joy radiated all the way down to his toes. He could feel the river wash over his feet, feel the heat of the sun warm his bare limbs, smell the heady mixture of bog and sea air that swept across the endless vista of grass. Jeremy didn't care one way or the other where he lived, but the city squeezed Simon. His clothes felt a little too tight there. People stood a little too close and sucked up his air. On the moors there was space to stretch and imagine. Their mother, who shared Simon's feelings for the place, watched him with a smile as the news was announced at the dinner table by their American father. The twins would go to their uncle's farm in Wisconsin for the summer, as usual, to acquire their annual dose of America, and then—freedom.

When school was out and whenever weather permitted, their mother took them onto the moors. Grace Vanderwall had grown up trekking the vast reserve, having been raised only a few miles away in the eighteenth century pile of stone that she had inherited. At home, she played the part of the executive's wife, hosting tea parties and dinners and wearing flowered dresses and high heeled shoes. But on walks with the twins, she plaited her hair, pulled on a pair of trousers and walking boots and shielded her face from the sun with a battered old hat. The moors transformed her, Simon thought. She was never more beautiful.

There were rules about the walks, which she had been drumming into the boys since they were small. You always took your ordnance map so you could keep track of the bogs. The grassy surface looked benign enough, but in that very uniformity lay its treachery. Set a foot down a mere yard from solid ground and you would be up to your hips in swamp. And then, of course, there was the mist. It was easy enough on a good day to become disoriented by the sameness of the landscape, but once the fog skulked in, which it could do unexpectedly, you needed a reliable compass and a hefty dose of good fortune to get out again. It wasn't for nothing that the famous Dartmoor Prison had been erected deep within the preserve to confine some of the country's most dangerous criminals. Escape attempts were rare since even prison was preferable to the terrors of the fog-veiled swamps and the quicksand that stretched for miles in all directions. It wasn't that you would be dragged down over your head the way they showed in movies, but you could easily go in up to your chest, and thereafter die of exposure. It wouldn't take long.

Simon's mother knew that he respected the moors and also that he had an uncanny affinity for finding the paths that others, Jeremy included, found practically invisible. It wasn't long before she was urging Simon to lead the way, and ultimately, in late autumn, she started letting them go on their own.

One Saturday, the following March, Simon woke early. He had planned to sleep in, but as he had left his window open the night before, woke to the sound of birds busily twittering. He lay still, watching the shadows of bare branches dance against the wall and breathing in the smell of sea and heather that rolled in from the moors. He could smell spring in the air, and felt too roused to loll around in bed. He dropped his feet to the floor, stretched, and padded to the window. For three weeks now, he had been leaving seed out at night on the narrow windowsill. The birds, mostly sparrows and wrens, would materialize all at once, as if someone had rung the breakfast bell. Chattering and fluffing out indignant wings as they vied for space, they would gobble up a seed or two, then fly off to the nearby walnut tree to await another turn. Simon had noticed right away that one of the sparrows was injured. She could fly well enough, but one leg was twisted and foreshortened. She landed awkwardly and had difficulty competing with the others who nudged her out of the way before she could grab a seed. Simon began shooing the others away for her. At first, the wounded bird had fled as well, but a few days ago she had remained behind. They sized one another up, she and Simon, two sets of eyes locked, one pair gray, one pair tiny beaded black.

"Come on," he had whispered. "Come and get it." She took a clumsy little hop. "That's right. Hurry up," he urged, "before those bullies come back."

And so she made it to the seeds, gobbling up four or five before flying off, rediscovering her grace. Simon had laughed out loud. And now, this morning, here she was again, not so far away from the others now, confident of her breakfast and blinking at him as if to say, "And just where have *you* been?" She ate her fill, and this time, came back again for more. "You little glutton," Simon said, and obliged her by tapping the window at the others.

Simon hadn't told anyone about his small triumph. He had always shared everything with Jeremy, or almost. It felt good to have a small secret of his own, something almost sacred. He loved waking up in the morning now to his communion with the damaged little bird. One day soon, he would try to convince her to perch in his hand. He tried to imagine the soft weight of her, like a breath. That would be something.

There was a hush in the house this morning. His mother's friend, Lily Adams, had been visiting from the States and there had been, as usual, a great deal of laughter. Each reunion, some new childhood memory would surface. Last week they talked of when they were both living in Cairo with their families. The girls had dressed in nuns' habits and hopped on the bus to the beach where they frolicked in the water and ate ice cream. Naturally, it had been his mother who acquired the outfits. She had lived next to a convent and managed to swipe the black robes from the daily laundry truck when nobody was looking. Simon enjoyed watching the two women revert to their youthful exuberance. On the other hand, he was perfectly content to see them off, Lily for America and her mother to meet his father in Brussels for the weekend.

Simon yawned and scratched his head, then padded down the hall to his brother's room. The house wasn't, in fact, totally silent: his brother's heartbeat was the usual muted accompaniment to his own. He stood a moment, watching his tousled twin sleep so peacefully with bare feet hanging off the end of the bed. Jeremy couldn't sleep unless his feet were unencumbered, perhaps to facilitate his dreams of chasing around the soccer field. The blankets were chaotic. For Jeremy, even sleeping was an athletic event.

"Rise up, rise up, and greet the day," Simon said.

"Go away," Jeremy muttered.

"We're off to the moors."

"It's winter. Go away."

"Not today it isn't." Simon yanked off the covers.

"Nasty bastard," Jeremy said, sitting up. "How do you propose to get there?"

"We'll take the motorbike," Simon said.

"On the road?"

"You've been practicing long enough."

"Yeah, but just on the back field." He thought a moment. "All right, I'm in," Jeremy said. "But if we get caught, nobody's ever going to believe it wasn't me who thought it up."

"Exactly," Simon said with a grin.

"You have a dream about birds?" Jeremey called over his shoulder on the way to the bathroom.

"Not exactly," Simon replied.

The boys worked efficiently through their routine, Jeremy making sandwiches while Simon packed knapsacks—jackknife, first aid kit, map. He finished up and glanced at the pantry wall for his mother's checklist. It wasn't there, only the square of tape that had adhered it. He made a cursory search and decided that she must have taken it down for some reason. He closed his eyes, visualizing it. He ought to know it by now—Mumma had been drilling it into them before every walk for years. Yes, he had everything. He was quite sure.

Out on the road, it was cool. But the thaw had been ongoing for almost three weeks now, and there was no denying the signs of winter's defeat. Trees were softly furred with new growth. The air was thick with the scent of wet earth. Simon, behind his brother, threw his head back and howled, "Wooo-hooo!" He was the one who always toed the line. Stepping over it this morning inspired a delicious thrill that buzzed agreeably in his solar plexus.

They parked the cycle at the foot of a popular trail. One of Simon's earliest memories was of following his parents along here for a Sunday picnic and being so close to the ground that the ferns seemed like a jungle. He was the intrepid explorer, using his stick like a machete to whack away at the undergrowth. Now he watched his brother hurry ahead, and grinned as Jeremy passed under the arch of a tree, jumping to touch an overhanging branch. He missed by a good foot. Jeremy always thought of himself as taller than he actually was.

Simon was surprised to see that the snow, except for patches here and there, had retreated almost entirely. Good news, he thought. His mother had declared the reserve off limits while its landmarks were buried. He and Simon walked north beside the river, which flowed in the opposite direction back toward the sea. The water tumbled raucously, rendering conversation impossible. The boys strode along in silence, working up a sweat. Three miles up, they arrived at a series of flat rocks. They shrugged off their knapsacks and sat staring silently at the water as they caught their breath.

"I wish I knew how to kiss a girl," Jeremy said. "I mean, a proper job of it."

Simon laughed. "Well, you've been working at it. At least that's what Charlotte says."

"True. But I have no technique."

"What about Rose?" Simon suggested, then wished he hadn't.

"She's in for heavier stuff than kissing."

"I saw her crying by the bridge." She had been all alone, Simon remembered, leaning against the railing. He had wanted to speak to her, dry her tears, share his sandwich with her, something, but not knowing quite how to approach her, he passed her by. Now he felt sad every time he looked at her. As if to cast off his own inadequacy, he stood and shed his clothes. "Going in?"

"You insane? I bet the ice just melted yesterday," Jeremy said with uncharacteristic caution.

"Just in and out." Simon was enjoying today's role as daredevil. He tugged at Jeremy's shirt.

Jeremy shook his head and stripped. The river was wide here and serene with small eddies dimpling the surface. The boys stood with their toes curled around the edge of the rock, gave a whoop and jumped in. The water was so cold that it felt gelatinous, barely this side of freezing. They splashed and shouted and were out within a minute. The rock was warm beneath them as they dozed, sunning like turtles, and gazing into a sky unmarred by the merest rag of cloud. For that bright handful of time, it seemed to Simon that there would never be a cloud, and that darkness would never fall again.

Simon got up and stretched, eager to move on.

"Want to go to The Circle?" Jeremy asked, in no particular hurry.

"Sure. We can eat lunch out there." Simon dragged his brother to his feet.

"Okay, but for once let me lead the way," Jeremy said.

The trail, perpendicular to the river, started out wide enough but soon became overgrown. After an hour of following the thread of a path, they reached the high ground and stopped to gaze out at miles and miles of open moors, the grass brown from the winter, rolling away in identical undulating hills as far as the eye could see. The land seemed to rise and fall in the wind, heaving gently like the surface of a vast ocean.

The sole landmark, in the distance, was Hag's Tooth, one of the many granite outcroppings called tors that stood like sentinels on hilltops across the open country. Hag's Tooth marked the outermost boundary for the boys' newly unsupervised trips whenever they ventured out this far. Once they set out again, however, Jeremy quickly became disoriented by the sameness of the rolling horizon, and it wasn't long before he made a misstep. Simon lunged forward, snagging Jeremy's arm and yanking him back onto solid ground. "Not that way," he said. "*Bog.*"

"Damn." Jeremy examined his foot, muddy past the ankle. He moved aside. "All right, genius. You first."

Simon, adrenaline pumping, edged past his brother on the narrow track.

They walked for a moment in silence. "Anyway, the ground is still supposed to be frozen," Jeremy grumbled after a while.

"We've had a thaw for almost a month," Simon said.

"You could be wrong once in a while, you know," Jeremy muttered. "It's so annoying."

Simon shot back over his shoulder, "Older and wiser," he said.

"Older by what, four minutes?"

"Eleven, to be exact." The protectiveness Simon felt toward his brother was nothing new, but the ferocity of it caught him off guard. The first time was when the twins were four years old, playing in the bath together before bed. When the water had cooled and their mother had pulled the plug, Jeremy began to scream. He scrambled to Simon, slipping and falling, soon face down in the water. Simon and his mother hauled the choking, rigid child out and wrapped him in a towel. Grace kept asking Jeremy what happened, and Simon knew in the way that he knew everything else about his brother. He saw the drain in his mind the way Jeremy did, a yawning black whirlpool sucking him down, and while Simon didn't feel the terror, he understood it with something beyond empathy.

There was the time Jeremy took that dive into a leaf pile from a tree in Wisconsin. Simon saw the grotesque angle of his brother's wrist as he stumbled up off the ground, and felt the sickening pain in his own. Finding Jeremy's suffering intolerable, Simon was always looking for how he might alleviate it. Simon's job was to be his brother's keeper; he did not resent it, nor did he wonder at its fairness. It was simply a fact of his particular existence, like looking older than his age.

The boys reached their destination at about noon. Nestled among low mounds, The Circle was invisible until nearly upon it, a clearing strewn with boulders arranged in rings of decreasing size toward the center. As with many other places on the moors, there was an atmosphere of magic here that gave rise to superstition. The twins liked to think of The Circle as a forum for the wild ponies that roamed the countryside. They had surprised a pair of them once, grazing here among the rocks.

Tired and hungry, they sat down with their backs against the sun-warmed boulders and ate, talking lazily.

"I'm sending you a postcard," Jeremy said. This was their code for the peculiar interchanges that often passed between them. They could "read" one another, almost as if they were looking at the same images on a screen or were flipping through the pages of a book together. As children, they had assumed that everyone did this until they realized that others found the process curious, even freakish. They had learned early on to keep it to themselves.

Simon closed his eyes. When on the receiving end, he found it worked better if he didn't try too hard. Shapes and colors gradually materialized, like a photograph in a chemical bath. "You still hungry, Jer?" he teased.

Jeremy laughed. "What did you get?"

"A platter. Blue ostriches on it. No, peacocks."

"And?"

"A steak the size of Aunt Lulu's backside. You want the other half of my sandwich?"

"Well, the steak's right, but I sent you a yellow plate with chickens."

"We're out of practice," Simon said drowsily. The sun was so warm, his belly so full, and the sweet air was intoxicating. He could feel himself drifting off, his thoughts mingling with Jeremy's, the physical space between them elastic. Maybe his mother was right—she said her boys were Siamese twins, who were joined by their souls.

It was the cold that woke Simon. He had no idea how long he had slept, but the sun had faded, the gray sky crouching over him like a threat. He leapt to his feet at once to shake his brother awake. "Jeremy, get up. We've got to go."

"Need a piss," Jeremy mumbled.

"Make it quick," Simon said, gathering up their gear. He considered. There should be another hour of daylight and nearly another one of twilight. They needed to head due west. Even if it got dark, they could just follow the compass reading. Once they got to the river, it would be easy to hug the bank and walk south. He rummaged through his bag, where he kept the compass in an internal pocket. It was empty. He cursed, turned the bag upside down and shook it. The compass was the third item on his mother's list, the list that wasn't there that morning. Simon had been certain that he'd remembered everything on it.

"Check your bag," he said to Jeremy. "The compass. I haven't got it."

"But you always have it," Jeremy said, as if observing that day follows night.

"Not today I haven't."

"Well, do we really need it?" Jeremy asked.

"Check your bag," Simon repeated, though he knew it wouldn't be there.

They were silent as Jeremy searched in vain.

"Bloody crazy," Simon muttered, referring to himself and his morning carelessness.

In minutes, they were back on the trail, the grass stubble dragging at their legs, the ground below oozing icy water. Jeremy looked as if he were sleepwalking, clearly stunned by the dramatic change in the day. Simon, on the other hand, was on full alert, realizing that the sky had drained the colors out of the landscape, blurring it to render it almost unrecognizable. He could still make out the dim smudge of Hag's Tooth, but only just, and set his feet on the course that he guessed would lead them to the river. No compass, dammit, dammit! Simon struggled to find the path, vainly hoping that his feet might somehow remember familiar ground.

"Did Mumma ever bring you out here when it was like this?" Jeremy asked.

"No," Simon said.

They walked in silence for a half hour, both boys with eyes focused on their feet in order to keep to the path. Finally, Simon looked up and squinted in the direction of Hag's Tooth. But what he saw instead halted him so abruptly that Jeremy slammed into him. Stretched across the horizon to the north was a massive cloud. It was rolling toward them like some gigantic rogue wave. Simon's heart leapt into his throat and lodged there, rendering him speechless. If only he had been able to see the path properly, they could have made a run for it. As it was, each footstep was halting, tentative, as he tried to find reliable ground.

"What?" Jeremy asked. Then he looked where Simon was staring. "What the hell is that?" he said.

"Blizzard," Simon said.

"No," Jeremy said. Simon was silent. "I thought it wasn't winter."

"I was wrong," Simon said. Neither of them referred to the earlier conversation about Simon's invincibility.

"Well, it looks like it's coming toward us."

"Assume it is," Simon said. "We have to get to the river before it reaches us."

"So pick up the pace." Jeremy gave his brother a little shove.

Simon struck out, hoping for the best. He remembered a story his mother had told him, about a birdwatcher who had gone out alone in May. A freak snowstorm had blown in and she barely got out alive. Simon knew that the weather was changeable out here, but the thought of a blizzard had never occurred to him, not on such a balmy day. And now, the white wall boiled toward them as if seeking them out. In no time at all, it was upon them. They were in the clear, and within seconds they were wrapped inside a nightmare. The wind howled in their ears making conversation virtually impossible. Snow, blowing sideways, tore at their clothes, pelted their faces, sought out every inch of bare flesh to scour with freezing needles. The boys, halted in their tracks, huddled together.

"I can't see six inches in front of me!" Jeremy shouted.

"Maybe it'll move through fast," he said into Jeremy's ear, which was already red with cold. But in his mind's eye, Simon saw an aerial view of the moors, blanketed impenetrably all the way to the sea. With the sickening surge of claustrophobia, panic closed around his chest. How was he going to get his brother out of here? The disappearance of Hag's Tooth and other markers erased his confidence of a safe route through to the river.

But one thing he knew. "We have to keep moving," he told Jeremy. "We'll freeze if we don't."

"Can't hear you," Jeremy said.

"Gotta go! Fast!" He started to take off his lightweight jacket.

"What the hell?" Jeremy shouted.

"Tie ourselves together. So we don't get separated."

"Bad idea!" Jeremy took Simon's jacket and replaced it around his shoulders. "Remember that birder lady Mumma told us about? It was exposure that almost killed her. We've got to try to stay warm."

"How will we keep together in this?" Simon asked.

"Believe me, Si," Jeremy said, using the childish nickname that popped out now and then. "I'll be right on your tail."

"You know I'm just guessing the way!" Simon shouted.

He and Jeremy stared into one another's faces for a

moment, hearing one another's thoughts: we have no food, no water, no protection.

"Let's go!" Simon yelled. "Stay close!"

They struck out again, with Jeremy just a footstep behind. It seemed uncanny to Simon that the storm never subsided for even a moment, just continued to batter them without letup. He kept in mind that it had come at them from the north and that the river lay to the west. They would find it eventually if they just kept moving with the wind slamming them from the right. The sound of it was horrendous, like a sky full of banshees, taunting them with their shrieking predictions of death. Simon covered his ears against them, but it was no use.

"Jer, better just hang onto me!" he yelled over his shoulder.

But there was no answer. Simon wheeled around. "Jeremy," he said into the white curtain. No answer. "Jeremy!" he called out.

He thought he heard a thin cry, off to his right. He started after it, calling. The sound came from behind him now, but further away. It might have been the wind. It probably was the wind. His isolation within the icy gale was total now. He began to sob, calling out for his brother over and over, only to be answered by the cruel howl.

He stumbled along for some time, his tears icing on his cheeks until they smarted. The ground had softened underfoot again, and it was slower going through the mixture of snow and mud. He tried to pick his way carefully, telling himself that if he could only but find Jeremy, he would be of use to him in some way. So, despite his exhaustion and fear, he kept moving. He even tried to be systematic. He could not have strayed far from where he had lost his brother. He would use the wind as a compass. Walking for thirty paces with the wind behind him, he would next turn directly to his left for another fifty paces, then left again, and once more until he had fashioned a rough square. Keeping up a constant barrage of shouts, he would then forge a new square by adding ten more paces to each side. Of course, the wind could be changing directions willy-nilly, and of course his earlier footsteps were immediately obliterated by the blowing snow. Of course a lot of things, but he was desperate for a plan, any plan at all.

He lost track of how many times he performed this futile exercise. His throat was raw with shouting, his legs felt like granite, and his feet had lost all sensation whatsoever. It had grown dark, and the only thing that kept him from lying down exhausted against the frozen earth was his belief that Jeremy was out there alone. He could feel his brother's need. Jeremy was a living presence inside him, but not like always before, when Simon could hear his brother's thoughts. Simon felt himself losing Jeremy into the cold, bitter night. Jeremy seemed still in his heart, in his mind's eye, but the image was vague. Simon's own fear must have been disturbing their communication.

And then, without warning, there was a kind of sigh across the moors and the storm passed off, as does a squall at sea. Just like that. Simon stood in wonder and watched its ghostly tendrils disappear away into the darkness. After the hours of bellowing wind, the quiet seemed supernatural, with a force of its own. Simon looked up. It was perfectly clear, with stars sprinkled by the millions across the sky. On the horizon, the moon was halfway risen, white, enormous. He turned slowly around, taking in the vista. Remarkably, there was very little snow on the ground. The storm had cleared up after itself, sweeping the drifts away as it moved off. Simon blinked, focusing on the silhouette not more than a few hundred yards away. Hag's Tooth. "Hag's Tooth!" he laughed bitterly. No more than two miles from The Circle! And then he started shouting: "Jeremy! Jeremy!"

There was an answer, a mere murmur. At least, with the great hulking rock so near, Simon had his internal compass back. He knew these dips and rises, knew them by heart. Jeremy was nearby. Simon knew it, could feel it in his pulse as he closed in on his brother, in the warmth that thawed his half-frozen body. "I'm coming," he told Jeremy. "Hang on just a little longer."

Simon found him in a little hollow that boasted one of the few trees in that area of the reserve, an aged cedar whose stunted form seemed almost human. Jeremy was up to his waist in bog. He was barely conscious. Simon approached him, stepping carefully, then lay flat against the ground with his face next to his brother's. "Jer," he said. "Wake up. I'm here now."

Jeremy barely moved his head but opened his eyes a sliver. "Screwed up," he murmured.

Simon could hardly believe that the ground had thawed enough to haul his brother down so deep. "Can you move your legs?" he asked.

"Stuck. Can't even feel them, it's so bloody cold."

"I'm going to try to pull you out."

"Won't work. Go away, Si."

"I'm not leaving you here," Simon said.

There was a long pause. Jeremy's eyes welled up. "Just stay away," he said finally. "They can't—look, they can't lose us both."

Simon didn't know what to do. And so he lay there, frozen in place, wishing the situation would undo itself.

"*Now*, Simon—before you freeze, too."

Jeremy was not exaggerating; his arms were motionless, his fingers chalky white. Simon picked up his right hand, blew on it and rubbed it, trying in vain to infuse it with even just a little warmth. Jeremy had begun to weep quietly. "Say bye to Mumma," he said. "Tell her ... tell her bye. That's all, okay? *Go*, goddammit!"

But Simon could not leave him. Not just yet. He knew about hypothermia, was aware of its stages. The bad news was that Jeremy was no longer shivering. Still, he was lucid and could move his head and neck. There would be lethargy and disorientation, then the final euphoria. If Simon were only able to find help soon ... He knew the odds were stacked sky-high against him, but he must not, could not, give Jeremy up to the lonely night.

Simon leaned in to touch his forehead to Jeremy's. Then, with an anguished cry, he tore himself away and stood up, his legs robbed of their strength, nearly collapsing under him. "Bye, Jer," he said, then turned and walked as fast as he could in the direction of the river.

*   *   *

After two miles had passed beneath Simon's feet, an image began to shimmer at the edges of his consciousness. He knew its source and stopped dead, afraid that if he so much as stirred, it might disappear. But it steadied and filled his mind suddenly in an explosion of light: two swans drifting side by side on the river, floating effortlessly in a shimmer of sunshine. And then at the flat rocks they parted, one remaining to watch the other slowly disappear downstream, leaving nothing behind but the jeweled surface.

"*Wait*," Simon whispered. "Oh, wait …" But that, he knew, was the end. A postcard from Jeremy. The last one.

OCTOBER

Most people agreed that the nerve center of Indian Wells was William and Lily Adams' dining room. It wasn't that there was anything so prepossessing about the space itself, nothing that didn't apply to hundreds of others within a fifty mile radius: a medium-sized room in a late Victorian stucco house. William's father, founder of Adams Manufacturing Limited, which supported the better half of the town, occupied a grand manor on eleven acres, but William and Lily were comfortable in their modest home, and saw no need to move even after William had taken over as president of the firm.

Tall windows hung across the south and west walls with window seats running beneath them, serving as both radiator covers and as perches for the friends and neighbors who showed up over the course of an evening. If there was surplus food—an extra breast of chicken, say, or a slice of pie—Lily Adams was quick to offer it. If not, no matter. William Adams' invitation to all who poked their heads through the door to "come in and watch the animals eat" was accepted without any expectation of handouts.

The multi-leaved mahogany table that dominated the room had been designed by William's father and built by a firm in Chicago at the turn of the 20th century. When you leaned your elbows on it, which everybody did, it spoke, not with a groan exactly, more like an apologetic protest, and its surface had certainly never seen a coaster in its life. Mrs. Adams didn't believe in them. Her attitude was that furniture was there for convenience, not tyranny.

Over the course of more than three decades, the following events, among countless others, transpired around that table. Millicent Terhune announced, at the age of forty-five, that she was finally pregnant and furthermore, now that her good-for-nothing husband had at long last performed his single essential obligation, she was divorcing him. Ferguson Dailey stepped gingerly out of the closet. Everyone had always presumed that he was gay, but Ferguson just kept on dating girls and breaking their hearts. Until, sitting at the table one winter's night, when the wind was howling outside and the radiators were steaming up the windows, he set his fork down beside a slice of half-eaten carrot cake, and declared with head bowed, "I'm going to tell you something. The fact is, I'm a homosexual." Tears slid down his nose and splashed onto his plate. Stella was off somewhere, so it was only Lily and William, who raised his hands to his wife in a helpless *what now?* gesture. Mrs. Adams went to Ferguson, put her arms around him and said, "But we know that, dear. And it's perfectly all right." His sexual preference having been validated at the hub of Indian Wells, there would be no more dating of girls and no more broken hearts on Ferguson's account, at least not female ones. Then, just last summer, Bob Withers had brought over his Labrador retriever and his brand new thirty-year-old second wife by way of easing the girl into a town that had closed ranks against him after he divorced poor SueAnn. The list went on and on. Some said that the Adams' dining room pulsed with some strange sorcery that provoked people to release their secrets, but a few of the wiser ones understood that it was not so much the room as the woman whose quiet presence illuminated it.

Amy Vanderwall's most memorable Halloween began as usual in her grandparents' house. Soon after arriving, Amy settled at that same dining room table to finish working on her streetcar. As far as she knew, Indian Wells was the only place in the universe where trick-or-treaters dragged the homemade trolleys behind them, and it was the reason she preferred to celebrate Halloween here instead of at home. She carefully cut out the squares that would serve as windows in the shoebox her father had donated. Next she would tape brightly colored Christmas wrap against the holes to create the illusion of stained glass. The intense afternoon light warmed the back of her neck as she worked and for a moment, at least, she forgot the ache in her mouth from having her braces tightened the day before. She was daydreaming, thoughts drifting about her head like the dust motes that danced in the sunbeams.

"How are you coming along?" Mrs. Adams asked.

Amy looked up and smiled at her grandmother. The two rarely made physical contact, and yet when Mrs. Adams was around, Amy somehow felt embraced.

"Almost done. I just have to tie the string on the end and put the candle inside." She held the streetcar up for inspection. "Do you think I'm getting too old for this, Gran?"

"Not on your life," Mrs. Adams said. "I'd go trick-or-treating myself if I didn't have dinner to fix."

"I'd like that," Amy said. "Who would you be?"

"Oh, someone very wicked. Snow White's evil stepmother, maybe, or Dracula. Now, would you give me a hand in the kitchen when you're done?"

"Be right there."

Now that Amy was almost twelve and plenty old enough to go trick-or-treating unchaperoned, she would sit down for an early dinner with the family before heading out afterwards with her friend, Wayne. She could already smell the roast beef in the oven. As soon as she was able to affix her candle stub into the center of the streetcar and make a hole big enough in the shoebox lid to prevent scorching, she slid off the chair and hurried into the kitchen. Mrs. Adams picked up an apron and tied it around Amy's waist.

"What are we making?" Amy asked.

"Most everything's organized, but I could use your help with the Yorkshire pudding batter. Oh yes, and the whipped cream. We'll just do them up and set them in the fridge for later on."

Amy liked watching their hands working side by side at the counter. Amy's were slender, the skin smooth as river stones. Mrs. Adams' knuckles had begun to swell with arthritis. There were prominent veins, brown spots from the sun, and a deep groove on her ring finger, carved by her wedding band.

"I liked your letter about the animals," Amy said.

Though separated by a mere two hours' drive, they often wrote to one another. This week, Mrs. Adams had reported watching out the window as the neighbor's dog, Earl, chased a cat across the lawn. The cat scrambled up a tree, which startled a bird who flew off with a squawk. Amy pictured the sequence of events as if they were illustrations in a children's book, the pages rigid cardboard: DOG, GRASS, CAT, TREE, BIRD.

"It would be even cooler if Mr. Trueheart started it off by running after *Earl*," Amy said.

"Well now, perhaps *Missus* Trueheart ran *him* out in the first place and I just didn't notice."

Amy giggled, imagining the timid Mrs. Trueheart flailing after her portly husband with a frying pan.

Once the Yorkshire pudding batter had been prepared, Mrs. Adams went to fetch some sugar from the pantry cabinet. "We'll just add a little to the whipped cream once it's stiff enough," Mrs. Adams said. She handed Amy the blender, knowing that she liked to make the cream thicken around the rotary blades.

"*Uh* oh," Mrs. Adams said, peering into the sugar carton.

"What's the matter?" Amy asked.

"Ants in the sugar," Mrs. Adams said. "Funny, this is a brand-new box."

"What can we do?" Amy asked.

Mrs. Adams deliberated. "Well, the store's closed by now. But we do have a sieve." She waited a moment, giving Amy time to think about it.

"Gran!" Amy protested, delighted.

"Mm, yes, those peaks are just about perfect." Mrs. Adams dumped some sugar into the sieve. It was dotted with little black insects.

"At least they're not moving," Amy said.

Mrs. Adams shook the sugar through the sieve. The ants, just slightly larger than the holes of the mesh, collected in a neat pile. She and Amy stared at them for a moment. "Do you think they'd be off limits to a vegetarian?" Mrs. Adams wondered. Just then, Amy's mother appeared in the doorway.

"What are you two up to?" Stella asked.

"Nothing!" Mrs. Adams and Amy answered in unison. Mrs. Adams hastily opened the cabinet under the sink and dumped the ants and the sugar carton into the trash basket.

"Amy, have you got a milk bottle?" Stella asked. "You'll need water for the streetcars."

"Sure, Mom," Amy said, her face red from the effort to control herself.

Stella gave her a long look. "And when you're done in here, why don't you come try on your costume." She went off down the hall.

"Oh, dear!" Mrs. Adams gasped, as she and Amy collapsed in laughter.

Finally, Mrs. Adams took a shaky breath, straightened her apron and said, "All right now, honey, you go on and take care of your costume. I'll finish up in here."

"Is it safe to leave you alone with the food?" Amy asked.

"A reasonable concern," Mrs. Adams replied.

"Do you notice that all the kids who've come to the door so far were wearing store-bought costumes?" Amy's mother asked at the dinner table.

"Yeah," Amy said. "Most of the people in my class bought theirs."

"Well, I think that's just so sad," Stella remarked. She had dark hair like her mother, though nobody could figure out where she got her dimples.

"Well, it's a new world, isn't it?" Mrs. Adams said. "Both parents are working these days, so there's nobody to bother with making a costume from scratch."

"*I* work and *I* make the effort," Stella retorted.

"Yes, darling, but not everybody is plugged into an electrical outlet every hour of the day."

"It's not a matter of energy," Stella complained. "It's a question of commitment."

"Uh oh," Simon said. "We're only on salad and she's getting her knickers in a twist already."

"Oh, quit it, you pompous old limey," Stella said, whacking him with her napkin. He grabbed the end of it and they started a good-natured tug-of-war.

"Yuk. You guys are so immature," Amy said.

"Pride ourselves on it, leafy greens," Simon remarked. His nicknames for Amy tended to follow patterns. Last month, they were celestial—"moonbeam" and "comet tail." She gathered that she was now in for vegetables.

Ordinarily, at this point on Halloween, Amy would be bouncing in her seat with impatience to get out the door. Strangely, though, tonight she felt like lingering, as if she might miss something by leaving. Perhaps it was because she had been told recently that her Grandmother Grace in England was terminally ill. At first, she had pictured her grandmother in a hospital bed in the middle of a railroad station with travelers hurrying past carrying luggage, though she knew perfectly well what "terminally" meant. She just wasn't awfully sad, really, which made her feel guilty. Whereas, had it been Gran ... oh, she couldn't even go there.

She looked around the table at her family. It was the first time she could remember a dinner with just the five of them at her grandparents'—no hangers on, no audience on the window seats. Not that she didn't enjoy the usual party atmosphere, but this somehow felt special. Besides, her grandfather was in a good mood tonight. You never knew when he might be really cranky, or lose his temper in some scary unpredictable outburst. Whereupon, Gran would go into her room and close the door.

"I brought a corpse for Wayne," Stella said.

"What'd you get him this time?" Amy asked.

"A beetle. It was on the outside windowsill of my hotel room in Mexico City. The window was jammed, so I had to fetch the hotel handyman. He thought I had a few screws loose. And don't you say a word, Simon."

"A word," Simon said, winking at Amy.

Amy found her mother profoundly irritating a good part of the time. Stella couldn't just *be*, but was always *doing*, rushing around taking care of the whole world's population. When she finally did sit down for a minute, her knee would keep bobbing up and down. Amy's father thought it was amusing—adorable, even, though it annoyed Amy no end. But then Stella would go and do something so kind, like this, bringing back an insect for Wayne's collection. For all Amy knew, Florence Nightingale had been really aggravating as well, always do-gooding halfway around the world.

"If you hadn't wound up fixing the international unwell," William Adams told his daughter. "You would have been a damn fine naturalist."

"Hm, yes," Lily remarked, "I seem to remember a story about a dead fish …."

"Oh, well, *that*," Stella said.

"Tell us, Grandpa," Amy said. She'd heard the tale before, but wanted to hear it again now, wanted to prolong this feeling of contentment: the savory roast beef, the battered surface of the dining room table, the gleam of her grandmother's chestnut and silver hair, the warm light encapsulating the five of them.

"These two had gotten engaged," Mr. Adams said, gesturing at Stella and Simon with the serving fork. It was hard to think of him as old with that muscular forearm and trim body, but then, he had had a heart "event" a few years ago. Everyone kept saying he was fine. "Your mother and I had a tennis game out by the lake," he went on. "Doubles, against Phil and Ryan what's-their-names."

"Mackin," Stella said.

"So, after we beat them, this one wanted to go for a stroll on the lakefront. And since I've never refused her anything …." He waited for Stella to protest. She obliged, and he continued. "She finds a fish washed up on the shore. *This* big." He held his hands a foot apart. "Weird-looking thing."

"It had wings or something," Stella said. "Strange fins, too. Anyway, I wanted to get it home where I could really study it."

"So we chucked it in the trunk," her father said, grinning at Stella.

"A minor complication," Stella explained to Amy. "We'd picked up the carton of wedding invitations that morning. They ended up sitting in there with the dead fish while we drove home, taking our time …."

"We stopped for mini-golf if I remember."

"Yes," Stella said, "and it got really hot that afternoon. In the nineties."

"And then we loaded up at the supermarket …"

"Amy, you have no idea," Mrs. Adams said. "When we sat down to address those invitations, well, we had to open all the windows and breathe through our mouths."

"Even the response cards stunk when they came back in the mail," Stella said.

"In her defense," Mrs. Adams said to Amy, "your mother has always been the ideal person to have around when there's a bat loose in the house."

Just then the front door opened and in walked a ghost pulling a streetcar nearly identical to Amy's. "Hi, Amy," Wayne called, his voice muffled under his costume. He stood in the dining room doorway. "You don't look exactly ready."

"Oh, come *on*, Wayne," Amy said. "*Casper*? And what is that? It's not even a real sheet."

"Mom wouldn't let me use one. It's a paper tablecloth." The boy pulled it up over his head, revealing a startlingly handsome face. He had perfect skin that was perennially tanned despite his utter lack of interest in outdoor activities that didn't include chasing bugs with a butterfly net. His idea of a good time was hunching over a magnifying glass with some spidery creature to study. His eyes were pale green, and fringed with dark lashes. Amy's mother said that Wayne was a nerd disguised as a movie star, which seemed about right. Although it was the nerd part that attracted Amy since the two were toddlers. After they hit the fourth grade, they alternated reading chapters of *Charlotte's*

Web to one another. She liked that he had cried at the end. His looks, she could have cared less about.

"Come sit for a second," Mrs. Adams said. "Dessert is on its way."

Wayne looked at Amy. He was rocking on his feet, anxious to get going.

"Mom's got something for you," Amy told him. Stella drew a chair up for Wayne and handed him a little cardboard box. "You can sit just for a second."

Wayne lifted the lid. "A fire beetle!" he exclaimed, dropping the box as if it were indeed aflame. It wasn't clear to Amy whether her friend was joking around or genuinely spooked. Wayne picked up a fork and poked tentatively at the creature.

"That guy's been dead a long time, Wayne," Amy said, and when he looked up at her in embarrassment, she felt like kicking herself.

"Which is just how we like them," Mrs. Adams said. "Dead as a doornail."

"Look at you," Stella crooned at the insect. "Aren't you a beauty, though?"

Amy cringed. Her mother was always getting into ridiculous conversations with animals, which was dopey enough, but this one was even dead. She had been known to talk to a log burning in the fireplace if it looked particularly lively.

Mrs. Adams smiled at Amy. "Who's in the market for dessert?" she said.

Amy got up. "I'll go, Gran." Amy went into the kitchen and began spooning the crisp out into bowls. How could she have missed that Wayne was afraid of bugs, even dead ones? Come to think of it, he always slapped on a liberal coat of repellant every time they went exploring in the woods. She had thought she knew everything about him.

She distributed the desserts—setting an extra generous helping in front of Wayne, who was explaining that fire beetles were so luminous that just one could supply enough light to read by in the dark. Amy went to fetch the whipped cream. Returning to the dining room, she stood in the doorway, enjoying the cool smoothness of the bowl in her fingers. Her grandfather was talking politics to Gran, who listened intently, chin on hand, while Wayne, satisfied that the fire beetle posed no threat, was pointing out to Stella various features of its underside. Amy's father gazed into the middle distance. It seemed a shadow had passed across his face, and that somehow the spirit of him had at that moment stepped out of the room. She wondered what he could be thinking about—certainly not sailing in his glider, which always made him smile. Since when had she found her family so absorbing, she caught herself wondering. But then the sight of Wayne's arm waving at her broke into her contemplation, the expression on his face a desperate plea to get away.

"Okay," Amy said out loud, her voice seeming tinny to her ear, like a bad recording. Was she was about to get her first period? Just the week before, her friend Roseanne had gone all sentimental and weird and that night it happened. Not that Amy was in any hurry. The entire production sounded pretty disgusting.

She went around the table dabbing whipped cream on the apple crisp. When she got to her grandmother, Mrs. Adams considered, then looked up with a smile and said, "No, thank you, dear. I don't believe I will."

Amy grinned back at her. I love you so much I could die, she thought.

Amy stood in front of the mirror in her Cookie Monster costume. She and Stella had labored for hours gluing pieces of blue crepe paper simulating fur to a blue pillowcase. The googly eyes were cardboard circles, the black eyeballs having wandered off in opposite directions.

"My God, Amy," Stella said. "You look like Mr. Wilcox." Amy's school principal, a humorless ex-shoe salesman, had a cast in one eye.

"Oh, he's all right," Amy said. Mr. Wilcox's conversation was liberally peppered with aphorisms, like how butter wouldn't melt in your mouth and how your chickens were coming home to roost. She had no idea what he was talking about half the time.

"Amy!" Wayne's voice shouted. "Are we going or *not*?"

"It's a great costume, honey," Stella said. "Are you sure you can see well enough through those eyeholes?"

"I can see fine," Amy said, grabbing her streetcar and her empty goody bag.

"Don't forget your fire extinguisher," Stella said.

Her mother's anxiety pricked her like a mosquito bite. She lifted up the glass bottle filled with water. Wayne was holding the front door open.

"Enjoy yourselves, peas and carrots," Simon called out, his voice somehow forced.

"Okay!" Amy called back. "I'll bring you some licorice, Grandpa! Bye!"

And they were out.

"I thought we'd *never* leave," Wayne said. "Cool bug, though."

"Gosh, what a perfect night," Amy said, glad she'd worn a sweater under her costume. The chill in the air was charred by the scent of burning leaves from a bonfire. Amy pointed two blocks down where some trick-or-treaters dragged their streetcars behind them, casting flickering colors against the darkness.

They set theirs on the sidewalk and lit the candles inside. Wayne had papered his windows all in orange.

"Nice," Amy remarked. "Who do you want to hit first?"

"Oxbow Street. The Piersons and Steins always have good stuff."

On their way at last, they glanced behind them often to make sure that their candles hadn't toppled over as the streetcars scraped along the crooked sidewalk. Wayne's paper costume rustled noisily with each step.

"I'm not sure I'm going to do this next year," Amy said, surprising herself.

"Come on, you can't quit on me," Wayne protested. "You're going to make me hang out with Jeff and Coleen? All they want to do is spray shaving cream on cars."

"Jeff's cousin has a crush on you," Amy said. They were both silent a while. "My water bottle's too heavy. I'm just going to park it here." She set her bottle down next to a fire hydrant.

"Me, too." Wayne put his down and they stood aside to make way for a batch of older revelers in dime-store masks who ran past, nearly toppling the streetcars.

"Anyway, there's nothing wrong with Mig," Amy said. "She's cute, and besides, she's my blood sister."

"So she's a cute vampire?" Wayne said.

"It has nothing to do with teeth. You just prick your fingers and then press them together so your blood flows into each other's bodies."

"Well, that's pretty stupid."

"Yeah, I guess."

They walked in silence for a while and felt the temperature drop. It wouldn't be many weeks before the snow flew.

"Girls are always falling in love with you," Amy said.

"Well, I don't know why," Wayne said.

"And all *you* can get worked up over is dragonflies and night crawlers," Amy said. "It's tragic."

They made stops at a dozen houses throughout the neighborhood, the last providing the promised licorice for Amy's grandfather. They were just heading back when Wayne's streetcar hit an uneven spot in the sidewalk and capsized.

"Shoot!" Wayne said. He reached down to set it upright. The candle had jostled free and ignited one of the windows. In an instant, the entire box caught fire. Wayne reached for it.

"Wayne! Leave it!" Amy cried. "We don't have our water …"

But it was too late. The blaze had leapt onto the boy's sleeves.

"Hit the ground!" Amy exclaimed.

Wayne stood still, immobilized. Amy leapt at him, tumbling him violently to the lawn beside the sidewalk. She heard the comic-book *oof!* as she landed on his slender frame with her full weight. She wrapped her arms and legs around him and rocked back and forth, rolling him along the damp grass until the flames were extinguished. They lay there for a while, panting.

"Jeez," Wayne said finally. "*Jeez*, Ame. Thanks."

"What's wrong with you?" Amy asked. "Were you *trying* to set yourself on fire?"

"I don't know," Wayne replied. "I wanted to save my streetcar."

"Yeah, and you just about gave me a heart attack," Amy said.

"Does this count to make you my blood sister?"

"'Til death do us part," she answered, with the appropriate eye roll.

Wayne thought a moment. "I think maybe it's 'til death us do part.'"

Amy had to laugh, which made her feel like she might start sobbing.

"I think maybe this may be my last Halloween, too," Wayne finally said.

"It could have been your last everything." Amy laid her head on Wayne's shoulder. After a while, they got up and started down the sidewalk. Wayne balled up the remains of his costume and stuffed it into the Allens' garbage can. Even so, he exuded the stale smell of a summer fireplace. At the next intersection the two split, setting off in their separate directions. Amy turned around to watch Wayne walk away from her, still clutching his bag of candy.

She was grateful for the quarter mile stroll to the house, which gave her the time to figure out what to say when they asked her how it went. She pictured Wayne, fire nipping at his costume, and was struck suddenly, as if slapped in the face, with the danger ever lurking in an ordinary day. She'd always known this in theory, of course. Her parents, her teachers, the newspapers and television were always sending out the message: *Don't Talk to Strangers! Look Both Ways Before You Cross!* She was aware that her mother's public health work took her into unstable territories, but the threats had always seemed abstract. And hadn't Stella always come home safe and sound? Tonight, though, felt like a sharp little stab of reality, an introduction to real vulnerability. It was scary on the one hand. On the other, hadn't she triumphed? Wayne had just stood there, paralyzed, but Amy almost reflexively determined a course of action and followed through on it. She was shaken enough that the *what-ifs* rose up unbidden. What if she hadn't known how to handle the situation? What if she had been too panicked to act? It was the kind of experience her mother sometimes reported about her work abroad, keeping her head when danger loomed—like the time there had been a gun battle going on outside her office in Kingston, Jamaica and her mother simply crouched under a desk as she continued with her phone calls. Feeling her breath catch in her throat at the memory of Wayne's predicament, Amy reminded herself of the certainty with which she had faced the flames and was comforted.

She had reached her grandparents' house and just as she had been reluctant to leave it, she was now hesitant to reenter. She dipped into her goody bag for the M&M's, her favorites, and shook some into her hand. From where she stood, in the light that poured out onto the lawn, the house seemed like a magnified version of her streetcar. As if she were watching a movie, she saw her parents captured in the frame of the living room window. Her father sat on the couch, elbows on knees, holding his head in his hands. Stella stood beside the couch, staring down at him. Her face was wet and she was speaking, but her father didn't respond. Finally, he looked up at her. Amy's heart twisted. She had never seen him look so terribly sad. Her mother held out her hand. After a moment, he took it. She drew him to his feet. Amy struggled to read her father's lips but couldn't make out what he was saying. Her mother was staring at him closely as if she, too, were laboring to understand. There was a long moment of stillness between them as they gazed at one another. Then her mother spoke. Amy heard the words through her eyes. *I adore you,* she was saying. Her father wiped the tears from her face and bent to kiss her, a long, deep kiss.

Amy lay under a quilt in the room that was always hers when she visited. Somebody had left the porch light on downstairs, and there was enough of a glow for her to make out the floral pattern of the wallpaper. Poppies, red ones. Mrs. Adams had asked Amy several times over the years if she wouldn't prefer to freshen up the room with new paper of her own choice, but Amy always said no. She liked the way the flowers looked, all randomly scattered.

They reminded her of *The Wizard of Oz* when Dorothy fell asleep in the field of poppies. Amy figured that flowers that made you feel like sleeping were a good thing for a bedroom wall, but tonight their spell eluded her. It seemed an eternity since she had hopped into the backseat of her parents' car for the drive north. She needed to flip through the vivid snapshots that her mind had accumulated. She remembered standing in the doorway of the dining room with the bowl of whipped cream in her hands. There they all were, her family and Wayne. As she pictured them, her heart began to swell. Under the cotton t-shirt that she wore to bed, it grew and grew some more, pressing against her ribs as if trying to escape its bony prison. She sat up on the edge of the mattress, her pulse pounding. She was crammed with feelings, full to bursting, exhausted and yet far, so far, from sleep.

She got up and went to the desk under the window and switched on the light. She took a notebook from her pile of schoolwork, opened it and stared at the blank page. *I can't hold it all*, she thought to herself. She chose a black pen; it seemed more serious than blue. "*My Last Halloween*," she wrote in the middle of a page, then turned to the next one. She sat for a minute. However to start? The only way, she concluded, was to smash the piñata, crack it open with a single blow and then pick through the contents a fragment at a time.

I came to my grandma's house today, she wrote. She stared at the sentence, not questioning that she had written "grandma's house," rather than "grandparents." The inadequacy of those seven words was humbling. There was so much history to be conveyed, so much joy and adventure and change and comfort, but they were a beginning, at least. They made her want to learn how to make her words say everything she felt.

When she was done, which was very early in the morning, she leafed through her pages. There were a lot of them, more than she had ever written all at one time, even in a letter. She knew that something important had happened to her. When she had stripped off her costume tonight, it was as if she had shed her skin, the person underneath someone quite new. And so she wrote it all down, taking special care with the culinary secret she had shared with her grandmother, Wayne's costume on fire, and finally the vision of her parents illuminated through the living room window.

She flipped back to the title page and stared at it. Something didn't feel right. The words *"My Last Halloween"* swam under her bleary eyes like three lonely fish in a pond. She picked up her pen again, and under the title, she wrote carefully, *"by Amy Louise Vanderwall."* She stared at it some more. Yes, this was better. But still she felt dissatisfied. She returned to the last page and read the final phrase: *"I have decided that I will be a writer."* She gazed at the sentence for a minute, then opened the desk drawer. There was a straight pin in one of the little wells inside. She took aim and stabbed her left index finger. Then she squeezed a drop of blood onto the bottom of the page. She pressed her right thumb hard into it, leaving a perfect imprint.

INTENSIVE CARE

William: 1960

William shoved off from the dock, leaving the family campground behind him in the woods. He slipped the oars into the oarlocks and began to row, dipping tenderly, respecting the silken surface of the water. During late September in the Adirondacks, dawn breathed over the lakes a mist tinted pink by the emerging sun, as the water, still warm from summer, met the chilly air. William slid in silence toward a rocky island bristling with fir trees and buttressed on its south side with an outcropping of boulders below which the fish, he knew, liked to feed.

But the first order of business had nothing to do with trout. He reached into the sack between his legs, retrieved a bottle of Glenlivet and cradled it reverently in his hands. It wasn't entirely his fault this time. He had passed plenty of liquor stores on his way north, slowing outside a few but ultimately summoning the grit to keep on moving. But up at the cabin, someone, perhaps William himself, had cached a half-finished bottle in the kitchen cabinet behind a stack of aging tuna fish cans. It was easy enough to convince himself. Fate must have had a hand in this, presenting that long-forgotten bottle to him like a prize. Furthermore, he was well outside what he called the sobriety zone—that is, within a hundred miles of Lily. In bitter moments of self-reflection, he defined himself as an "out of town drunk." Then, as now, the mere image of his wife's face shamed him. He stared at the label for a moment, considering. But then … he was alone, after all, with no one to witness his degradation. Didn't he deserve a reward for months of self-denial? The familiar rush of helplessness consumed him, but excitement, too. He knew the joy that would flood him in those first moments. Quickly, he lowered the bottle, opened it, and took a swallow. The irony of it, that such heat could extinguish its own fire. Gratitude swam through his veins. *Finally*.

Back when he entered college, William had discovered alcohol as a corrective to some missing element in his physiology. When he drank, something clicked into place. It didn't make him crazy drunk, just contented, normal, like other people. But after almost four years of drinking steadily, he began to have blackouts. He woke, trembling, every morning, needing a drink. So he just stopped. It was agony, the loneliest time of his life. He would ask himself in a swamp of sweat how it could be that what you needed most was the worst thing for you. But by the time he met Lily, he hadn't had a drink in six months.

The decades had passed and every now and then, he had screwed up, usually well outside the sobriety zone. He told himself that there had always been, if not an excuse, an explanation. He had one today, too: it was his fifty-first birthday and he was all by himself. For the second year in a row, Lily had gone to visit a friend in London. This time, though, she had phoned to extend her stay indefinitely. He knew why. Not that she would ever talk about it. A year ago to the day, William had made a catastrophic mistake. He kept waiting for his wife to forgive him. It looked now as if it might never happen.

William slung the sack behind him, rested against it, and gazed up into the brightening sky. Mercifully, the liquor had begun to do its what-the-hell job. He drifted into a pleasant alcoholic reverie. While the pale celestial bowl above him eased into blue morning, he reflected on his two great loves. Alcohol was one. And Lily.

The first time he saw her was at the summer wedding of a Yale classmate. There had been cocktails on the lawn of the Greenwich estate. William stood sipping ginger ale and chatting idly with Tom Templeton, the best man. With graduation behind them, Tom was exhilarated about his new job in finance. William watched his friend's narrow face with curiosity; what about banking could produce such euphoria? And then William caught sight of a young woman. She was standing in the garden nearby. Flowers rose about her knees in polychromatic splendor, as if placing her on a lavish display. She was tall, slender, and straight with a thick chestnut braid that fell to the middle of her spine. She wore an ivory dress of some ethereal fabric that draped her body simply, elegantly. All the other girls, with their shapeless knee-length dresses, wore their hair in pageboys and bobs. Standing among them, this young woman seemed to have stepped out of an Edwardian novel. He had never seen anyone like her.

Feeling his gaze on her, she turned toward him suddenly, shading her eyes with a hand. Their eyes met. "Who *are* you?" William murmured under his breath.

Tom swiveled to determine the source of the interruption. He laughed. "Forget it, Billy boy. She's engaged."

"You know her?" William asked.

"I've met her. She's the bride's cousin. Name's Lily Brooks, I think."

"Lily," William echoed. "Excuse me, I'll be back."

"And that's her fiancé she's talking to!" Tom called after him.

Even as she returned to her conversation the young woman's posture changed, as if she detected William's approach out of the corner of her eye.

"Hello," he said, holding his hand out to shake that of Lily's startled companion. "Hate to break in, but the bride apparently needs her cousin for a moment." He took Lily's elbow and drew her away. She was just two inches shorter than he. He'd hardly even need to bend to kiss her.

"Who are you?" she asked, an echo of William.

He felt it, and pulled her closer. "William Adams."

Her eyes were the kind that changed with the light. Just now they were green. There was amusement in them, and not a little alarm. "And you're a friend of the groom?" she asked.

"Classmate."

At this moment, a tow-headed child came careening up to her and, wailing, buried his face in her skirt. Lily bent down and cupped his face. "What is it, Georgie?" she asked. She smoothed his hair with tender fingers.

The boy sobbed out a tale of injustice that was incomprehensible to William for the heart-rending sobs that punctuated it. Lily listened attentively, then wiped Georgie's cheeks with the hem of her skirt. "Do you see that man dressed like a penguin?"

Georgie sniffed, nodding.

"He has ice cream for the children on that tray," she said. "I think you'd better have some, don't you?"

Thinking it over, the child nodded again, no sniffling this time. "Will the penguin give it to me?" he asked.

"All you have to do is ask him." Lily kissed the little boy on both damp cheeks, and off he scampered. She straightened up and turned her attention back to William, who was wondering how many children he would have with this girl. He gazed at her in a kind of rapture.

"Where's my cousin?" she asked.

William shook himself out of his trance. "Are you really going to marry that fellow?" he asked.

"Vanessa didn't ask for me, did she?" Lily said. She was wrapped in light, the air around her pulsing with colors, with the sounds of birds. He could sense the grass growing up around their feet, smell its sweet aroma. They were at the center of the universe. He could feel the sun's eye on them.

Just then, Lily's aggrieved fiancé rushed up, having perhaps made the same deduction as Lily. William, adrift on memories so many years later, could not put a face to him. Did Lily ever think about him, ever imagine what her life might have been like if she had married him, especially now, with William turning out to be such a disappointment?

The ceremony had transpired on the lawn. William's arm, where Lily's body had warmed it, continued to vibrate long afterwards like the surface of a struck gong. Unable to spot her in the seated crowd, he assumed she was behind him somewhere.

Then, as the minister began his tribute to the happy couple, William began to sneeze—not decorous little *ah-choos*, either, but a spectacular series of eruptions. Suddenly there was an echo of daintier sneezes—five of them in quick succession—and William turned through pouring eyes to see Lily pushing past her young man with a handkerchief to her face. The minister had halted in his tracks. The spines of the bride and groom had stiffened. William escaped his aisle seat to follow the stricken girl. He caught up with her at the parking lot, where she was leaning against a car. She sneezed again, as if in greeting, and he answered with a paroxysm of his own.

"The peonies ..." she stammered. "I should have stayed out of the garden. I *know* better ...." She gazed at William over the handkerchief and began to laugh. "Oh, dear, this is awful!" she cried, and then he started in. Soon they were both red-faced and weeping from a combination of hilarity and pollen.

It was the first time he heard her laugh. William was to learn that Lily's laughter could breach her remarkable composure, a phenomenon that only happened otherwise when he made love to her. Those tantalizing glimpses into her unguarded self undid him totally, captivating him even all of these years later.

William took her hand as they searched for his car. They located it, finally, and got in.

"I thought the parking lot would be *safe*," she protested, wiping her teary eyes with a handkerchief.

"It's this breeze," William said, "strewing the pollen everywhere."

They were quiet for a moment, recovering.

"This is fate, you know," he said.

She smiled. "So romantic."

"You're not going to marry that fellow, are you?" he asked again.

"He's telling everyone I am."

"But will you?"

"I haven't promised. But I might."

"Why?"

"Because he's a very decent man, and I like him immensely."

"That's not reason enough," William said.

"Well, why does any couple get married?"

He took her hand. "Because they can't bear being apart."

"Isn't that a bit extreme?"

"No," he said.

"Well, I'm fond of him."

"Oh, Lily Brooks."

"Oh, Will Adams," she said, smiling.

The way she had shaved his name down to its diminutive made his stomach do a flip. He loved everything about this girl.

"He should take your breath away," William told her. "*I* can do that."

"I suggest that might be the allergies."

He leaned in then and kissed her. He felt her body relax against his for a second before she pulled away, staring at him with eyes wide. "That was wicked of me," she said. He reached for her again but she held him off. "You're a dangerous man," she said.

"Better than boring."

She smoothed her dress, calming the wrinkles as if the gesture might be enough to salvage her self-possession. "That's unkind."

"Careful is no way to live."

"It's one way to live."

"It's why you have to marry me."

His campaign began there. Lily resisted at first, if only out of compassion for her earlier suitor, but William was relentless. He believed that he could win her, and so he did. William was competitive, always had been, in the futile pursuit of his father's approval. He'd won the golf tournaments at the club. He excelled in tennis. His grades were good. Nothing William ever did, however, had earned more than a grudging grunt from his father. Until Lily. After William brought her home to meet his parents, Harris Adams began to regard his son with curiosity, if not wonder, perhaps even something close to respect. Before long it became clear to William that the old man was more than half in love with her himself.

• • •

William was surprised to notice that he had consumed about a third of the scotch. He was never certain how he was going to respond to alcohol, but even so he was feeling remarkably strange—not drunk exactly, but oddly detached. A breeze had sprung up to roughen the surface of the lake, chasing the mist away, and the light was now so pure that everything seemed almost too sharply defined. He felt he could perceive every needle on the shoreline pine trees, and yet they seemed to inhabit another dimension, as if he were dreaming them. He knew what those trees looked like stripped of bark, could smell their sticky resin. He loved wood, a reverence he had shared with his grandfather—his grandfather who had, in fact, founded the furniture company that supported the town in which William had grown up, the town in which he still lived. His mother had given him a box of Lincoln Logs once, but he found them inelegant and built his own model house from scratch, with a roof fashioned from tiny slate shingles and a pebble chimney. If only his grandfather had lived a little longer, he and William might have preserved the quality of workmanship at the factory. But his father was as indifferent to the grace of a finely crafted chair as he was to the company's history. It was all about money to him. Down to the very end, before he died, he sold the business to a national conglomerate. William now functioned as little more than window dressing.

He raised the bottle to his lips, noting the strange numbness of his hand. His fingers seemed the size of bananas. He fumbled briefly with the lure he had chosen for his rod, then gave up and took another deep swallow. He dozed off until nausea woke him. Still, his hands felt steadier. Trying to ignore the sickness in the back of his throat, he forced himself to sit up and tie his fly onto the leader. He stood, and with practiced skill, whipped the rod using his wrist, then watched as the line and feathered lure settled light as a whisper.

Harris had taken William fishing once when he was around five. It had been a momentous event for the boy to spend time alone with his father. William had gone worm hunting the night before to fill an empty coffee tin with wet dirt and night crawlers. Charged up by the same anticipatory thrill of Christmas morning, he woke long before dawn and lay waiting.

After they finally pushed off from the dock and reached their first fishing spot, William sat jabbering away in the bow with his line in the water. His father ignored the chatter at first, then remonstrated, and finally, unable to silence the rapturous boy, grabbed a night crawler and popped it straight into William's mouth. It occurred to William now that his father had been stuffing worms in there ever since, most notably during board meetings when William had had the temerity to offer a new idea.

He took a sip of scotch against the phantom taste and noticed with irritation the distant purr of a motor in the distance. It was the mail boat, making its morning run down the lake. He had slept longer than he thought. Though the water appeared flat as a plate to his eyes, the boat seemed to be riding swells beneath his feet. He saw little explosions of light as if a flash camera was popping too close to his face. The nausea kept rising and falling in his throat. There was a sharp tug on the line. Dizzy, William's legs gave way and he sat abruptly. He struggled against the weight of his catch—this was no rainbow trout. A snag, maybe. And then a jagged pain ripped through his chest, sending him sprawling into the bottom of the boat. He vomited, blacked out, came to and blacked out again. Through it all, he clung to the rod, clutching it to him as he lay fading in and out. Somehow it seemed important to hang on, as if the line at least might tether him to the reality—he was simply a middle-aged man fishing on a beautiful morning.

Suddenly, the line snapped and William himself split in two. Half of him lay senseless in an agony too fierce to bear, while the other was catapulted up into the air, and then back above the family campground on shore where he hovered like a gull. He could hear the moaning of the person in the bottom of the boat, a muted accompaniment to the more captivating scenario unspooling below.

There was a party underway. People carrying cocktails and hotdogs strolled along the soft pine-needled paths that knit together the collection of rustic buildings scattered through the woods. There was a gathering around the barbeque pit and another one down on the dock, which held a bar and a buffet table. William realized, from his aerial perspective, that it was the company's annual summer outing. He recognized certain people—Grandfather in his fishing hat, his mother sitting on the edge of the dock with her women friends, dangling her bare feet in the water. She looked young, maybe thirty.

He zoomed in on the front stoop of one of the cabins, the one they called Blackbird, where his parents always stayed. William had often slept there on a cot when he was a toddler. It smelled of the wood fire that burned in the Franklin stove on chilly Adirondack nights. Just then, a boy wearing William's favorite cowboy shirt came up the path and let himself into the cabin through the screen door. William followed him in and saw him stop short beside the bureau. His face registered first bewilderment and then what looked like horror. William gazed now at what the boy saw: Harris, lying in the bed, naked from the waist down. Straddling him was Mrs. Hewitt, their neighbor from Baldwin Road, breasts bare, denim skirt hiked up over her thighs. They were moving together in some strange rhythm that was kind of like dancing. There was something very wrong in that room. The boy knew it, though he couldn't have said what it was. He made a sound, and the two froze.

"Get out of here, William!" Harris shouted, registering the boy now. "Get the hell *out*."

"Mother wants you," the boy said.

"Oh my God," Mrs. Hewitt said. She yanked at a blanket to cover herself, but not before the boy had seen one of her large brown nipples. Something about it disgusted him.

The boy turned on his heels now, and William watched him run, stumbling over roots along the path. Tears streaked his face. He was fast, and reached the dock in no time. William wanted to stop him, but knew it was impossible. The boy ran straight to his mother, who was standing now with a drink in her hand. William saw him tell her, saw him point back at the cabin. Everyone on the dock heard him and turned to listen. Now the guests backed away from his mother, as if she were contaminated. She remained alone, rigid, her eyes closed, until two of her friends remembered themselves and went to support her. William could no longer see the boy. It was as if he had simply disintegrated.

The man in the bottom of the boat cried out, and William slipped back inside him, inside the pain, which was almost a relief, and so he remained until he woke up in the hospital.

He was sedated, but even so, he understood that he was at St. Timothy's. There were tubes and wires attached to him, and a machine emitted the reassuringly monotonous chirp of his pulse. The pain was more manageable now, merely a dull ache across his chest. He turned his head carefully to either side, looking for her, but she was not there.

His eyes drooped, and suddenly he was curled in the backseat of his parents' Ford. He wore a jacket over the cowboy shirt, and it was dark all around him except for the erratic beam of the headlights on the trees as the car hurtled along the pitted road. His mother was in the passenger seat. She was crying. William had never heard that sound before. In fact, he had only once seen a grown woman weep, but that was in a movie, and it hadn't been nearly as terrible as this. His mother could barely get the words out between her sobs. "*How could you?*" she was saying, over and over again. "*With all those people there. With your child there. How could you?*" William supposed that he must have been the "child." It hurt him that she did not use his name. He had known right away that down on the dock he had done an unforgivable thing. There had been the stricken look on his mother's face when he told her, the color sliding visibly from her cheeks, and she had swayed as if she might fall right into the water. And the sudden hush of the guests, staring at him with their mouths open. "I'm sorry, Mama," he whimpered from the backseat of the Ford, but she didn't hear him, or maybe she did.

"I'm sorry, Lily," he said to no one, aloud in the hospital room. Sorry for all of his transgressions, one in particular. He was so thoroughly, desperately sorry.

He slept a little. Then a nurse came to check on him. She had a pleasant square face and a competent manner. "Do you have pain?" she asked.

He nodded. "My wife?" he said. He had to squeeze the words out between dry, swollen lips. His throat felt raw.

"She'll be here soon," the nurse said, and then she did something to his IV bag to set him adrift again.

The sensation confused him, floated him as if he were back on that boat again. Each time he docked into consciousness, he looked for Lily but she never came. Only the nurse showed up, again and again. As it was always light in the room, it was impossible to discern the hour. Days seemed to pass, maybe weeks. "Don't you ever get to go home?" he asked the nurse.

"Never," she said with a smile.

"Where's my wife?" he asked.

"On her way," she assured him.

But in his morphine dreams, Lily was being interviewed on the television affixed to the wall opposite his bed. "And will you be going back to your husband then?" the newscaster asked. He had a British accent.

"No, I'm afraid not." Lily was young, and dressed in her wedding gown.

"Why is that?" the man asked. "You know he's most terribly sorry."

"I tried to get beyond it," Lily said. "I just couldn't, that's all. My own weakness."

How typical of Lily to blame herself, William thought, as the dream screen faded to black.

A year ago, on the day he turned fifty, William had been at a trade show in Chicago. He had complained to Lily that hanging around with a bunch of furniture executives was hardly his idea of how to celebrate. Wouldn't she please take the sting out of it by coming with him this time? He could tell she was torn. Her childhood friend in England was in a bad way as she approached the anniversary of her son's death. William pointed out that it had been more than five years since the tragedy, but Lily just looked at him and said, "I know, Will, but think of Stella." Stella, their funny, difficult, loving, precious daughter. What if they were to lose her? He understood and told Lily to make her reservations.

William found trouble on his very first night in Chicago. Even though he no longer drank, he still enjoyed hanging out at hotel bars when he was on business trips. Often there was a heightened camaraderie at such places, people gathering far from home to shed the tension of travel, gear themselves up for professional functions, or simply chase away their loneliness for an hour or two. William still remembered the man's name— Frank Marshall, from some little town in South Carolina. He was built like a linebacker, with a thick neck and huge paws. He was an encyclopedia about orchids, of all things. Somehow over the course of the conversation William let it slip that it was his birthday. Afterwards, William would look back and obsessively attempt to reconstruct every word, every nuance, to explain what happened next. After all, he had stood at countless bars over the years, had made it through barbeques and cocktail parties and weddings, and managed to survive them all cold sober.

He remembered that Frank had ordered William a drink to celebrate the half-century mark. A general fuss had been made. The song had been sung. Had William ever protested? He could not recall. In any event, he had succumbed, and soon felt himself dropping once again like a stone through a vacuum, flailing with nothing to grasp at, nothing to slow his descent, no way to save himself, getting high by falling down—and down he plummeted, with more drinks after the first, toasts exchanged with his new best friends, and an hour later, he was in his room, drinking steadily from a bottle he'd purchased from the bartender.

William stood in the dark at the hotel window, watching a dramatic thunderstorm play out over the black vastness of Lake Michigan. Through the alcoholic haze, he contemplated the magnitude of attaining the half-century mark. What had he achieved, really, in all those years? His occupational goals had been modest enough: to improve and expand upon the accomplishments of his grandfather. William's ideas were sound, even inspired, yet they had been obstructed by his father each and every time. It took William a decade of frustration to figure out that his suggestions were far more likely to be implemented if they emerged from someone other than himself. Ultimately, the profitable rustic furniture line was established, and the cost-cutting computer system was installed, with others receiving the credit and the raises, while William told himself that it was his contribution that counted, not the paternal acknowledgement. Bastard.

As for his marriage—Lily had been a part of his life for more than half of his fifty years. Shouldn't the jagged panorama of his early passion have worn down by now, by the thousands of passing days into a softer, more forgiving landscape? It was, after all, what he noticed in other couples: that gentle domestication. But for Lily, he still yearned. Seethed. Raged. Adored. In return, she was unfailingly kind and ever thoughtful, but how could it be that in all these years, Lily had never once told him that she loved him? He had delivered the declaration to her on any number of occasions, moments when it just spilled out, partly from the joy of releasing the admission when his heart was so full, and partly in the dim hope that perhaps this time she might respond in kind. But it was always the same.

"I love you, Lily, so much," he would say.

"I know you do, Will," she would reply with a tender smile.

What the hell was that, anyway? he wondered at that hotel window, bottle in hand. She made him feel like a favorite old sweater you've worn until the elbows wear through. The more he thought about it, the angrier he got. The fuse lit, he felt the familiar heat rise in his chest. God *damn* it, anyway. He knew he was going to throw something. Sometimes he had enough self-control to reach for a pillow instead of a lamp, sometimes not. Pitiful how half the time he couldn't even remember what set him off. A couple of months ago, he had slammed his fist into the kitchen wall, then simply stood there staring at the dent. That was going to be a nuisance to fix. He wished he'd chosen a painted surface rather than wallpaper.

Memory surfaced now, and with it the shame. It had been the laundry. One of Stella's red socks had gotten into the white load, staining one of his favorite golf shirts an uneven pink. He had thrust it at Lily, shouting like the fool he was, before stuffing it into the garbage along with the melon rinds and discarded eggshells. He thought of Lily's face, and the alarm in her eyes— even fear. She would go to her room after those explosions and stay there a long time. He dropped his head into his hands. His palms were still hot now and pulsing with the need to strike out, but he remained very still, breathing carefully until he was calm enough to reach again for the bottle. It was a quarter empty. At least he hadn't broken anything.

The wind was howling outside the hotel now. Rain swept sideways against the window as if William, sheltered in his room, were traveling through the fierce night on a high-speed train. Where could he be bound for in such a hurry? His head was aching and he began to feel a little sleepy. He thought about forcing himself to pour out the rest of the whiskey and put himself to bed. But there was a sound, a knocking barely audible over the violence of the storm. If only he had ignored it, but how was he supposed to anticipate that one tiny splinter of time was going to alter his life forever? There should have been bolts of lightening crashing into the room. Thundering tympani. *Something* to alert him that he was standing on the brink. Certainly not this hesitant little tap.

He went to the door. A young woman stood there trembling, drenched. "I'm sorry," she said. "I heard your TV on and thought … thought I wouldn't be waking you."

His TV was not in fact on, but no matter. "You're soaking," he said. She was pretty, but more than that, she was giving off a live current, as if her body had somehow harnessed the storm. He wondered if he'd get a shock if he touched her.

"I think my lock is broken next door. If I could just call housekeeping for someone to come …? I can't get in and I'm so cold." At this, she broke into sobs.

William felt a lump form in his throat and reminded himself that he was pretty drunk. But this girl was breaking his heart. He drew her into the room and sat her down on the couch. He fetched some towels, wrapped one around her shoulders and gave her the other to dry her hair. Gradually, her weeping quieted.

"I'm so sorry," she said. "What a display. I should have gone to reception. I guess I felt paralyzed or something."

"Would you like some of this?" William asked, holding up the bottle.

"Yes, please," she said.

He poured generously, and as she drank, the story came out. Of course, it was all about a man.

"I guess I thought if I walked out in the storm," she said finally, "the rain would just wash him away."

She was shivering and William could see goose bumps wherever her flesh was exposed. The bath towels were too damp to be of any use now. He sat on the cocktail table opposite her, brought her closer and rubbed her arms to warm them. She leaned forward and kissed him. Her mouth was soft. It was not Lily's mouth. After all these years. Oh, Lily.

"It's my birthday," William said. What he meant was, despite everything, that kiss had felt like a gift.

"Which one?" she asked.

Out of vanity, he was reluctant to tell her. "Fifty," he admitted after a second. The shock in her face disarmed him. She must have been in her thirties.

"Do you feel different," she asked, "turning fifty?"

"Besides drunk, you mean?"

"You don't act drunk."

"Sometimes that happens," he said, remembering times when he had behaved like a cartoon wino, stumbling and lurching and howling at the moon. No predicting. "Yes, a little different, maybe," he said.

Getting up that morning, he had checked himself out in the mirror to see if anything had changed. But all he saw was the same bony face, deep-set hazel eyes, a beat-up nose from years on the playing fields, thinning gray hair, which he kept cropped short. He could never understand what it was about that face that women found appealing, but for some reason they did. Over the years, he had developed a ritual around any overly flirtatious woman of making repeated references to his wife. But he didn't seem to be doing that tonight.

"Different how?" the girl wanted to know.

For some reason, perhaps because he had been working on a crossword on the plane, he imagined a long string of letters, the alphabet stretched out like a track into the distance. He was strolling along it, stopping here and there, to celebrate at "b" for "birth," to mourn at "d" for "death," to heal at "h." At fifty, there were actually more letters behind him than ahead of him. "m" … "n" … "o" The journey more than halfway done; he would soon glimpse on the horizon not so far ahead that final letter: "z." For "Zero." Nothing. Oblivion. "Seems kind of like a time for reflection," he said to the girl.

Yes, he was lonely. And wounded that Lily had once again forsaken him. The liquor was warm in his veins and now here was this lovely girl with warm lips beside him. Her hair, dryer now, sprung into a glorious tangle of brown curls. She picked up his left hand to examine the wedding ring.

"I suppose your wife doesn't understand you."

"Actually, she does," William said. "I don't understand *her*."

The girl held William's hand to her heart. "You can do me a big favor," she said.

"What's that?" William asked.

"Hold me."

He took a shaky breath.

"Nothing more. I just really would like if you could hold me."

With scotch-soaked logic, William thought about how Lily's friend in the U.K. really needed *her*, and here was someone who needed *him*. If Lily could put someone else's needs ahead of his, after all, why then shouldn't he feel free to comfort a stranger who happened to be suffering? He held out his arms. She smelled like the rain.

· · ·

Afterwards, he saw that she didn't want to leave, but William needed her to. He needed her to disappear without a trace. In his memory, she would be more phantom than reality, floating in a mist of single malt. He was glad he didn't know her name. In fact, he rarely thought of her after that night, except now and then during an electrical storm, and of course when he got back home and her black lace panties fell out of his suitcase along with his laundry. The girl hadn't seemed the type to walk around without panties. And how had he missed them when he swept up his dirty clothes from the floor the next morning?

Lily had come to get him in the yard where he had been raking leaves. Her face gave nothing away. "Follow me," was all she said.

He had had the absurd notion that a family of mice might have taken up residence in her sweater drawer again. But then she pointed at the bed. She had arranged the panties neatly on the quilt. They looked alive, as if they might begin to crawl across the mattress like some gigantic malignant spider. He reached for her. "Lily …" he had said. "I can tell you …." But what could he have possibly told her? She had interrupted him anyway.

"I don't want to hear about it," she said.

"Can I just …?"

She held her hands up in front of her face, fingers fanned, shielding herself from the sight of him. "No. Don't say anything. Not ever, William. I mean it. *Not ever.*" She turned her back on him and walked out of the room.

For weeks after that, she was quiet around him, around everyone, in fact. She was unfailingly considerate, but often enough he could see in her face that she had been crying. So could Stella, who asked William what was wrong with her mother. Time slipped by, and at last the day came when she at least smiled again, and some time after that, her laughter returned. He had been terrified to touch her, but in the spring she had come naked to their bed. He knew she wept afterwards, but they resumed their regular lovemaking.

If anything, Lily grew more beautiful as she aged. He would look at the wrinkles in her face and feel privileged to be the resident witness of her evolution. And now she was gone. Oh, the sorrow of her absence. How futile to imagine that the drug dripping into his veins right now could relieve the terrible pain of losing her.

And then, when he awoke, she was there. She sat beside his bed, her eyes fastened on him, as if she had been watching him exactly like that for days.

"I thought you weren't coming," he whispered.

"I just got off my flight," she said. "The first one home."

"But it's been days, weeks …."

She smiled. "No. They brought you in just yesterday."

That seemed impossible. "Did they tell you what happened?"

"You had a heart attack," she said.

He took that in. "Oh," he said finally. "All right."

"All right?" she echoed.

"My heart, Lily," he said. "I must have worn it out, loving you."

ASUNDER

Stella had been in love with Simon her entire life. It felt even then, at fourteen, that the ingredients of him had always been in her head, just waiting to gel into flesh and blood. She remembered thinking when he finally showed up that summer day: *oh, yes, there you are. What took you so long?*

She used to amuse herself sometimes by thinking about what single word applied to people she knew. Amy's friend Wayne, for instance, was *bugs*. She felt confident that insects were the last things he thought about before falling asleep each night and the first things when he woke up in the morning. The word for her daughter, Amy, was just as easy: *writing*. Amy had a regular job now, in the foreign rights department of a publisher in the city, but that wasn't who she was. Often during a conversation, her eyes looked vacant and you knew that she was listening to those other people she'd invented rather than to you. Stella's own word was *Simon*. And Simon's, of course, was *Jeremy*—presenting the tragic little love triangle that had simmered beneath them for years like some poisonous polluted river. Stella had always hoped that it would dry up over time. Instead, it had boiled into a torrent that had finally swept Simon away from her four years ago. Stella had collapsed into a bereavement of singular torment, intensified by Simon's proximity in the same town. She would make a trip to the post office, praying that she would not see him, but grieved all the same when there was not so much as a glimpse of him. Rarely, there was a sighting. It was always the same: Simon, wraithlike now, fled before the moment of collision. How she missed all the most specific and familiar aspects of him—how his big toes didn't match, for instance, how the leftover English accent surfaced when he was tired, how summer streaked his hair—these were the things that taunted her.

She realized that he was suffering more than she could ever imagine. And yet, she resented the fact that the better part of her life, from adolescence on, had been spent in response to Simon. Why, after all, had she dedicated herself to working with desperate populations in faraway lands? Surely it was in large part an escape from the pain of her early conviction that Simon did not love her and never would. He was fond of her, certainly, and wrote her long chatty letters. A blue airmail missive would show up in her mailbox and she would think, maybe this time. She tried not to hope, knowing that it was fruitless, but she couldn't help herself. She would save the letter, unopened, for hours before reading it, teasing herself, or perhaps putting off the inevitable pain. Either way, she would succumb in the end, taking care not to tear the fragile paper. A deep breath, and then she was with him as he unraveled the past few weeks of his life, often flippantly describing the details of a love affair gone wrong. She succeeded in forcing herself to wait at least a week to reply, but failed to throw his letters out. She had them still, in an old hat box of her mother's that smelled faintly of lavender.

Back in their youth, Stella and Simon had seldom gone more than a few months without seeing one another. Their mothers were friends and there were visits on both sides of the Atlantic. Stella lived for those times and yet they tortured her. She was confident that *he* did not lie awake thinking of *her* face, that saying her name did not feel like a prayer in his mouth, that the sound of her voice did not reverberate through his body like the vibrations of a guitar string. So she took the veil, a secular nun, renounced romance and made herself useful.

And then there was the Christmas miracle. It happened in her parents' house upstate at Indian Wells one December when she and Simon were in their twenties. Simon had taken a job in New York as an interviewer at an employment agency.

It was something to do until he figured out his future, but he enjoyed the work, each day a series of dramatized short stories, each client's predicament more fascinating than the last. Stella was between projects, but with the Democrats in power in Washington, funding had loosened up. There was a grant pending on a women's health center in the Ivory Coast that looked like it might come through.

As usual, Simon had been included for the holidays. It was late on Christmas night and Stella's parents had gone to bed early, overcome by the glut of too many gifts and too much good food. Simon and Stella sat side by side on the couch in the glow of the tree lights and the fire. Corny holiday music slid from the stereo as they traded narratives about their exciting new lives as participants in the real world. Bing Crosby began to sing, "*I'm dreaming of a white Christmas ...*" Simon set his wine glass down, stood and offered his hand to her. "Come Stella, we've never danced together."

She could still remember the absurd acrobatics performed by her heart as she stood and moved into his arms. Aware that she was blushing, she hid her face against his shoulder. They were both tall, he over six feet and Stella only two inches shorter. In all these years, there had only been quick friendly hugs between them, but now she became aware of how her body aligned with his—chest, abdomen, hips—how the arc of her shoulder nested into the hollow below his own.

"*... where the treetops glisten and children listen ...*" Their steps slowed until they were merely swaying in time to the music. Stella unconsciously held her breath. Surely he could feel her heartbeats pummeling him like little fists. Simon tightened his arms around her and it was as if all the hours and days and months they had shared over their lives were caught between them in their embrace. Then, as the song drew to a close— "*And may all your Christmases be white ...*"—he held her away and looked into her face. Silently she wondered, would he tell her yet again how she was his best friend and that he could never manage without her? Because she could not bear that, she remembered thinking. She would not have seen him again afterwards. It was too hard.

"I'm in love with you, Stella," he said.

Each word a thundering crash from the heavens. Stella staggered a little, closed her eyes and replayed them in her head. She had surely misheard him.

"I have been for a while," he said. "I just didn't know it."

Tears collected on her lower lashes, trembled there, and spilled down her cheeks. Simon brushed them away with his thumbs and cupped her face.

"Dance with me again," she said.

"*I'll be home for Christmas …*" sang Bing.

Simon smiled and gathered her back into his arms. "*… you can count on me …*"

Throughout the ensuing years, until Simon finally slipped away from her, she would wake in the morning wherever she was and think of him, of how he loved her, and often of that very night when he had first told her. Those few seconds would remain in her memory as the birth of her complete self, of what she could only think of as her soul. Sometimes it astonished her, that the memory would be so fresh, as if it had occurred only days ago. She would have thought that it would fade and ultimately lose its impact, like a favorite song played over and over until its power to transport is utterly worn away. But no, she would think of him and feel herself levitate to hover halfway to the ceiling, buoyed by joy and gratitude. Often, Simon would put music on the stereo after dinner and dance with her, a ritual that amused Amy to no end. Stella would melt into his arms. "I'm drunk," she would whisper. "I'm drunk with love."

That January after Simon's avowal, they had driven through a snowstorm to Carnegie Hall to hear Vladimir Horowitz. Stella had been so captivated that she felt woozy and had to remind herself to breathe. After the many encores, Stella and Simon stood applauding in a kind of trance. When the stage was finally empty, Simon turned to her and said, "Let's get married."

"Okay," she said. "When?"

"Next week," he said.

"Okay," she said again.

"Excellent." He grinned at her.

"I think you should probably kiss me," Stella said.

It had to have been the longest kiss in human memory, Stella thought. By the time he finally released her, just about everyone had filed out of the hall.

They walked out into a soft winter night. A light snow was falling, blurring the hard edges of the city and transforming it into a black-and-white photograph. Simon had hold of her around the waist. Stella plucked the arm of a young man hurrying past with a backpack. He turned.

"We're in love," she said. "We're getting married."

"Right on," he said, and continued on his way.

"Hey, let's get some hot chocolate," Stella said. "Over there." Hip to hip, they crossed the street and slipped into the coffee shop on the corner of Fifty-Seventh Street and Sixth Avenue.

"One coffee, one hot chocolate," Simon said to the waitress.

"We're getting married next week," Stella told her.

"Nice," the waitress said, clearly less than delighted with their order and the tip it suggested.

"We're very much in love," Stella said.

"One cheesecake and a rice pudding," Simon added.

Somewhat mollified, the waitress gave them a half smile and moved away. Stella got up immediately and squeezed herself onto Simon's lap.

"I love that I've known you since you were a kid with scabby knees," Simon said.

"And now I'm a *grown-up* with scabby knees," Stella said.

The snow had started to come down in earnest as they walked back to Stella's apartment. A couple hurried toward them. They seemed engaged in an argument, but Stella, undaunted, stopped them anyway. "This man proposed to me tonight," Stella told them. "I said yes."

"Oh, fuck off," the woman said, and pulled the man away down the street.

Stella stared after them and back at Simon. His eyes were

watering from suppressed mirth.

"Anyway," Simon said after they had recovered. "You didn't say 'yes,' you said 'okay.'"

And so it was that they embarked on a romance that lasted nearly two decades, until the grasp of that early tragedy reclaimed Simon. His withdrawal froze Stella out. When he entered the room, the temperature dropped. At the dinner table, he sat like an ice sculpture, silent and staring ahead. In bed, his forced "good night" was often the only sound she had heard from him all day. One night, she stared at his rigid shape beside her and thought, as she had countless times before: Talk to me about your brother. Give him to me, to us to share. But she knew from long experience what such a plea would elicit: not just silence, but such a naked expression of pain that she would have to avert her eyes at the sight of it.

So instead she said, "Please, Simon. Can we at least talk to each other?"

He lay still for a moment. "I hate that I'm doing this to you," he said finally, then got up and went into the den. He slept on the couch thereafter.

She couldn't remember who had initiated the final split. It was something they both knew must happen. In no way did that conviction ease the agony of his departure, however, and there had been several times when Stella had weakened, usually with the excuse that reconciliation would be good for Amy. The last attempt had been a year ago. When he phoned her back, he sounded almost like himself. A flicker of hope lit up in her head, and she gripped the steering wheel tight as she drove to the diner, "their" diner, where they had spent countless hours talking, arguing, teasing. She had begun to go into labor at that place. They had joked that this was why Amy's favorite foods came straight off the menu.

He was already there when she arrived, and stood to kiss her cheek. A bad sign, but she shoved her foreboding aside. After all, he had showed up.

Their old waitress stopped by. "Good to see you," she said, grinning at the sight of them together after so long. "Same old, same old?"

"That'd be fine," Simon said.

There was no color in his voice. Fear began to creep into Stella like some sort of furtive, burrowing insect.

"Amy over the flu?" Simon asked.

"Yes," she replied.

"I'll call her," he said in that dead voice.

Amy was to some small extent an exception to Simon's shutdown. For his daughter, at least, he made what must have been a supreme effort to communicate, however minimally. Stella was grateful for it, but nonetheless could not help resenting that what he could do for Amy he somehow could not do for her.

"You phoned me," Simon said.

"Yes. I guess I was wondering if maybe …" she stammered, "… if maybe we could give it another try. For Amy's sake."

"Amy's sake," he echoed, staring at her blankly.

What had this soulless man done with her husband?

"Why did you answer my call?" she asked.

He didn't reply. The waitress set down two corn muffins, with raspberry jam for Simon and honey for her. No longer looking so cheerful now, she slunk away without a word.

"I'm sorry, Stella," he said finally.

"You shouldn't have come," Stella whispered.

"No. It was wrong."

"You almost sounded happy on the phone," she said.

"Happy," he repeated, as if he had never heard the term, his eyes focused on a spot somewhere near her right temple.

"Don't you feel *anything*?" she asked.

"Yes." His eyes gripped hers now. They were filled with despair.

"Is the therapy helping at all?"

"I don't know," he said.

"Where *are* you?" she asked.

"In hell," he answered.

"Is there nothing, then? Nothing I can do or say to help you?"

He just stared at her for a moment, and then his gaze

slipped away from her again. They sat in silence for several long minutes, the muffins untouched.

"Don't do this to me again," Stella finally said. "Not ever."

She left him there. Whenever she felt the compulsion to reach for the telephone, to share with him perhaps some tidbit about Amy, she forced herself to remember the diner and steel herself against him—or, more accurately, to that specter inhabiting Simon's skin who had no more to do with the man she loved than a figure in a wax museum. Her Simon was gone, replaced with a tormented soul whose pain was clearly beyond her capacity to imagine or to ease. She was a widow.

RAIN

Lily & Simon: 1985

It was barely light when Mrs. Adams awoke, jarred by the eerie song of the muezzin calling the faithful to prayer. It was happening more often these days, but then she'd heard that old memories sharpen with age even as recent events blur into faded scraps. Even last week seemed like a patchwork quilt that had been laundered too many times.

If she were to keep her eyes closed to stay in Jerusalem, she could almost smell the meat roasting in the streets, hear the donkeys braying, the church bells clanging. What a glorious city, with its luminous stone, its desperate history. How lucky she had been to spend so much of her childhood in such a place.

She could not remember Jerusalem without thinking of Grace. They had met at the English-speaking school perched above the city on the Mount of Olives. Although small then, and shy, Lily had nevertheless been placed a grade ahead of her own age group. All the other girls seemed so sophisticated to her—especially Grace, with her confident style and clipped accent. Lily was the only American, and the sound of her flat Yankee "a's" seemed to her ugly and crude. She never understood what it was that had made the English girl seek her out, but that very first day, Grace had marched up to her and asked, "Why are you here?"

"My father's a minister," Lily had explained. "A missionary. In the Presbyterian Church."

"I thought missionaries went out into the jungle," Grace said.

Lily shrugged. "Maybe because he's kind of a businessman missionary."

"Well, *I* certainly don't believe in God," Grace said.

Lily burst out laughing. She had never heard anything so outrageous in her life, and half expected Grace to be struck by lightning on the spot. Later, Lily would learn that Grace had been convinced Lily's father was a spy. An intriguing thought, but then Grace was always full of fanciful notions.

The girls spent two years together in Jerusalem, and then, as luck would have it, another two in Alexandria, Egypt. But after that, years would go by without their seeing one another.

Over the course of Mrs. Adams' long life, she had found that there were certain friends who would put themselves on the line for you, practically from the first meeting. They were few and far between, of course, but at the end of even the first conversation with such a person, it was as if they said, "A pleasure to meet you. Be sure to call me if you need somebody to step out in front of a truck for you." Grace Vanderwall was one of them, and today was the anniversary of her death.

Ultimately, Grace's son, Simon, had married Stella, Mrs. Adams' daughter. She knew that Grace's death had exacerbated Simon's slide into darkness and his withdrawal from his wife and child. There had been a divorce. Still, Simon was Grace's son. Furthermore, Mrs. Adams was fond of him in his own right, and worried about him—never more so than on sad anniversaries like this one.

She sat up in bed, taking inventory of her arthritic joints. Rain was coming, no doubt about it. The barometer would rob her of ambition on days like this, but she had determined to pay Simon a visit, and visit she would. Nothing wrong with her that a little aspirin and some exercise couldn't fix. She would see her dentist this morning, have lunch and a quick nap and be on the road by three. She would make an adventure out of it, packing her overnight bag and staying at the motel she had frequented when Amy was little. Certainly, she would not phone ahead lest Simon invent some persuasive reason why she should stay home.

Lunch was the same as breakfast, a half bowl of cornflakes

and Sanka. She merely grazed these days. Her father had held that there were two types of elderly: "shrinkers" and "swellers." Mrs. Adams knew she really ought to gain weight, but she was clearly a shrinker, and large portions made her stomach ache. She lay down on the couch to doze for a bit and when she awoke, she declared herself quite perky, particularly for someone pushing eighty.

She looked into her handbag, which held several hundred-dollar bills she intended to leave with Simon. As an old lady, bestowing money was her privilege—what else was she going to do with it now if not help out her children? Over the years, she had saved up what she regarded as a small fortune. She had never held a real job, hers being to deal with William and the household. He was what her mother called a "handful." Feeling that she was entitled to some sort of compensation for that, Mrs. Adams had opened an account on her own, setting aside a little every week of "just in case" money, as she called it.

She poked her head out the kitchen door for a weather check. The day had turned out quite steamy, one of those September afternoons that might as well have been August. Mrs. Adams took the measure of the billowing white clouds that now filled the sky and, determining that they could easily lose their temper as the hours wore on, dropped an umbrella into the Oldsmobile before climbing in. How had it gotten to be four o'clock already? She felt equal parts excitement and anxiety. It had been a while since she had driven any farther than the supermarket, and it was a good hundred and fifty miles to Simon's. Still, she had made that trip plenty of times over the years. Simple enough, really: a straight shot east along the Mohawk River and the canals to Albany and then south to Hudson. It would be a pleasant change of scene, and it would be a chance to reassure herself. She hadn't seen hide nor hair of Simon for six months.

The passing streak of rural New York scenery and the ribbon of asphalt stretching ahead into the distance encouraged her mind to wander, which didn't help her driving any. She was an uncomfortable driver, and erratic in her speed, ranging from a crawl to greased lightning. Occasionally, a car streaked past her on the left or worse, on her right—horn bleating, but she was used to that. She stared at her hands on the steering wheel. It was startling how much they looked like her mother's, now that the knuckles were swollen with arthritis. Someone ought to write a biography of a pair of hands, she thought, especially a woman's. She would read a book like that.

It was pleasant to let her thoughts drift. She imagined Simon's face, handsome in its angular way, with his mother's same gray eyes, haunted with sadness from that early tragedy. "Superman eyes," Stella called them. They could burn holes in you, she said.

The thing about Simon that Mrs. Adams had appreciated most was that he "got" Stella. With her delirious highs and crushing lows, she could be baffling, a challenging child to raise. It always took twice as long to get anywhere with Stella in the car; she was always shouting, "Stop! Stop! Do you see that *view*? I have to take a picture!" William hated to pull over once he'd put the car into gear, but Mrs. Adams always obliged. They had a closet full of boxes crammed with indistinguishable photos. Squint hard enough and you might make out the backside of a deer disappearing into distant shrubbery. Or perhaps it was just a rock. Stella had celebrated the experience of seeing it, whatever it had been, and passed her exuberance along to you, her outsized capacity for joy like a gift.

Mrs. Adams had always worried that Stella would go down in flames in some spectacular nervous breakdown, but Simon somehow allayed her apprehension. His disposition in those days was even-keeled, and he observed Stella with a grin on his face, as if he were standing curbside at a wild parade his wife was leading. It wasn't hard for Mrs. Adams to understand; her husband's intense engagement in life had attracted her in much the same way. He could be outrageous and infuriating, but at least he made it harder for her to sit back and watch the world go by, which was her own inclination. She remembered the time they had gone to the closing party of a favorite restaurant. William had met her there following his weekly bowling game and had his ball with him. As the farewell speeches grew ever more lugubrious, William started bouncing his leg restlessly. Finally he got up, cleared an alley down the center of the room, placed some empty wine bottles at the far end and sent his bowling ball flying for a perfect strike. Who else would do such a thing? And when, on a fishing trip, William had snagged the dead body of a reveler who had perished in a drunken boating accident only three nights before, Lily was not the least bit surprised. Of course it was William on the front page. It always was William.

Simon, like Mrs. Adams, wasn't a big "doer," as William Adams complained, but neither was he passive. For one thing, he made *appreciating* an active art. And when Stella paid for her ecstasies with the corresponding plunge into misery, he knew instinctively how to handle her. Mrs. Adams remembered the first time she witnessed this dynamic firsthand. Stella had been on one of her early assignments, setting up a women's health center in Tanzinia. She had become attached to a toddler who subsequently died in her arms. She contained herself for the remainder of the trip only to collapse as soon as she walked through the front door at home—wailing with grief, her sobs interspersed with apologies. As always, Mrs. Adams had stood by feeling helpless, horrified at this extravagant display, indeed, even a little guilty: how had she failed so dismally to equip her daughter for the realities of life and death? William was no help; he just threw his hands up in the air and went off to play golf.

But when Simon had arrived for dinner, he immediately absorbed the pitiful tableau and scooped Stella into the living room where he simply held her. She struggled against the embrace at first, but Simon only held her more firmly and murmured, "It'll pass, Stella, it'll pass." Mrs. Adams had stood in the doorway and, incapable herself of such equanimity in the face of her daughter's hysteria, watched with wonder and gratitude.

And that was why it was so sad when the light went out of him, when all he would do was sit for hours in front of the television. Simon had always hated television.

•　•　•

It seemed no time at all before the exit sign for Hudson popped up. Judging that a mile to the ramp left her plenty of leeway to overtake a pesky slowpoke of a truck, she passed it, veered back into the right lane and slammed her brake pedal before she could rear-end the station wagon directly in front of her. There was a chorus of horns—enraged, alarmed—that suggested to her that perhaps it might be wise to take a daily practice drive around Indian Wells just to keep her hand in.

She would invite Simon out to dinner. That dispiriting new apartment he rented—well, not so new now after five years— would simply never look homey or lived in no matter how long he inhabited it. It had taken him two years even to unpack the cartons from the move, and even that, she suspected, Amy had been primarily responsible for. Mrs. Adams would stop off at the little airport Simon mostly frequented that was on the way. It had used to scare Mrs. Adams half to death once he got his license and started taking Amy up with him. Later, after he began to lose interest in life, the airport became about the only place he seemed even halfway engaged. He left his job as a residential real estate broker, an occupation he had always enjoyed. He liked the stories, he told Mrs. Adams. Every homeowner or buyer was a potential saga. Now he spent most days either aloft or on his back under skimpy looking planes with a wrench in his hands.

There was no one in the airport office, so Mrs. Adams headed directly to the barn that served as a hangar. The hulking girth of Norbert Ewing, the airport's manager, mechanic, and troubleshooter, loomed into sight from behind an all-purpose snowplow tractor. Where, Mrs. Adams wondered, had he managed to find overalls in such an enormous size? He stuck out an oil-covered hand, thought better of it and offered Mrs. Adams a heart-melting smile instead.

"Changed your hair," he said.

"And you," Mrs. Adams said, "are the first and only person to notice, you improbable man."

"Drove yourself down, did you?" Norbert asked.

She nodded proudly. "I suppose I was having an adolescent episode."

"He's up," Norbert said, gesturing skyward. "Late, too."

"How late?" Mrs. Adams asked.

"Hour or so."

A couple of folding beach chairs had been set out beside the single runway.

"Sit?" Norbert said.

He might have been a man of few words, but the worry in Norbert's face was plenty eloquent. She sat down and scanned the sky for the dot that would indicate her son-in-law's plane. *Ex*-son-in-law, she reminded herself. The clouds were towering now, their bellies angry and dark.

"Does he do this often? Stay up there too long?"

"I've told him a few times before, too many ..." Norbert cut himself off. "There." He pointed out at the sky with a huge square finger, but Mrs. Adams couldn't see a thing except roiling thunderheads. What a ridiculous day to choose for a trip. Perhaps she was becoming delusional, like her bridge partner. Mrs. Adams was forever taking her own mental temperature in this regard. The last thing she wanted to be was a troublesome old dodo, and there was a perfectly comfortable apartment complex just down the road from her house. Ah, now she saw it. The dot was growing more substantial now, and soon enough was accompanied by a low buzz. But wasn't it dropping too fast? She glanced at Norbert, whose eyes were stuck to that plummeting smudge in the sky. She stood up.

"That doesn't look right," she said.

"I've told him," Norbert said again.

They waited in silence. Mrs. Adams had not realized until then just how late it had become, the sun by now a peevish orange glow just above the horizon while the clouds boiled overhead. Funny, that saying: *my heart was in my mouth*. Yet it was exactly right. Mrs. Adams could barely swallow against the throbbing lump. But time did some strange slow cartwheel until finally the little airplane slid onto the far end of the runway and taxied to a stop. Norbert stalked over, hands on his hips, and waited for Simon to emerge. The big man stood there, solid as a tree, emitting a series of indistinguishable grumblings.

Mrs. Adams thought she heard the word "docked," or was it "fucked?" Simon, his face inscrutable as ever, listened while Norbert had his say and then turned on his heel. Glancing over her way, he recognized Mrs. Adams. His face seemed to light up for a moment. "Lily," he said, coming to greet her with a kiss for each cheek.

"It appears that you're in the doghouse," Mrs. Adams said.

"He worries too much."

"Well, I hardly blame him!" she said. "I certainly thought you were going to crash." By now, it was actually dark. She felt a fat raindrop splash on her wrist.

"What brings you down here?" Simon asked.

"An adventure," she answered. "I'm taking you out to dinner and staying overnight at the Eagle's Nest."

She watched as the joy, only moments old, slid off his face. It never lasted for long, since time together required interaction and Simon did not want any part of that.

"I'm not much on dinner," he said. "I sort of snack all day."

"I'd like to fatten you up, but if you're not hungry, you can just watch me," she said. She wanted to slip her hand through his arm, but there was a shell encasing him, as if he were enclosed in that stiff, clear plastic they sold things in these days. "Maybe you'll develop an appetite on the way to The Post House," she went on. "You used to like a nice big steak."

"You're awfully bossy," Simon said with a trace of a smile. It gave Mrs. Adams a pang. Simon's grin used to always transport that melancholy face into a delicious display of gleeful creases. And his laughter was straight out of a comic book: *ha ha ha*! You couldn't hear it without chiming in.

"I don't see your car," she said.

"I have a motorcycle now, but it's in the shop. Norbert was going to give me a lift."

"A motorcycle!" One more way to eliminate yourself, she thought. "You drive, then." She handed him the keys. "Don't smash into anything."

There was a gigantic crack of thunder just then, a piercing report that left Mrs. Adams covering her ears. She looked up at the sky as the drops began to pelt them in earnest, weighty enough to feel like hail. Simon grabbed her arm and hurried her along to the Oldsmobile. He slipped in behind the wheel and shoved the seat back to accommodate his longer legs. The side mirror was splintered where a rock had been flung up against it. Simon shook his head.

"I know," Mrs. Adams said. "I'll attend to it next week."

"I remember Amy asking you if they called it an Oldsmobile because it's so old."

Mrs. Adams smiled. Those were better days when Amy, Simon and Stella were bound in a union that seemed unassailable. They even had their own odd language, with made-up words. Mrs. Adams couldn't keep track of them all, but she remembered that *frith* meant "love." It was used a lot.

Simon pulled out onto the rain-slicked road. Absent of traffic, nobody with any sense was out here now. The wind had picked up, buffeting the car with torrents of rain that rendered the wipers nearly useless. Mrs. Adams grabbed hold of the door handle for security, and several times found herself jamming an imaginary brake with her foot. "My, it's dark as a pocket," she said.

Soon, they were forced to a crawl. Simon leaned forward to squint out the windshield. "It's like driving underwater," he murmured.

"I can't even see if anything's coming," Mrs. Adams said. "We could easily hit somebody or get rammed from behind."

Simon was quiet, but he did that thing with his jaw where the muscles clenched into a knot. Suddenly, there was a brilliant flash of light, and in that moment of eerie illumination, Simon spotted the tree that lay across the road just ahead. Thunder boomed and rolled around them even as he swerved, the car spiraling out of control. Mrs. Adams continued to cling to her door handle. Even as her brain told her that they were in peril, she found herself simultaneously experiencing a thrill of excitement that set her heart to pounding as they spun around and around on the drowning road. She could have sworn that she actually laughed out loud, thinking, *What a way to go!*

After what seemed several minutes of this wild ride, the vehicle catapulted headlong into the ditch. Miraculously, they landed only slightly atilt. They sat in stunned silence for a moment, shaken by the impact.

"Not quite the sort of adventure I had in mind," Mrs. Adams commented, the percussion of rain on the metal roof nearly shouting her down. She touched Simon's arm. "I'm just glad you're not up there in that plane," she said. The sad smile he gave her by way of response was not entirely a comfort. She wanted to embrace him, wanted to hold him on her lap and rock him as if he were a little boy. That pain in his eyes was something she recognized, though no one in the world knew of her own long-ago descent into the hell of depression, of her own yearning for release—really, for death.

It had been about a year after her baby died. Now Stella was four, and into simply everything. The little girl thought it a great joke to run right out into the street, and loved climbing things, the higher the better. She even crawled out her bedroom window sometimes, to perch on the narrow ledge. The physical and emotional toll of keeping such a child safe simply exhausted Mrs. Adams. And on top of it, William was in nearly daily conflict with his father. He came home ready to tear things apart in frustration. One night he flung a stewpot clear across the kitchen. Beef ragout slid in a gooey mess down the wall as Mrs. Adams and Stella cowered beside the refrigerator. William was instantly mortified, as always, and cleaned everything up, but his violence terrified Mrs. Adams. What was to prevent him from unleashing it on her some day—or worse, on Stella? That night, she had slept on the daybed in Stella's room. Actually, not really slept, just stared up at the ceiling William had decorated with little stars that glowed in the dark. She wished they were real and that she could float up into the infinite black sky and be delivered into oblivion. It felt cowardly to long for death, but her despair was that suffocating, as if she were buried alive in cement with no prayer of escape. Her heart thudded, taunting her with its sturdy beat. She was young and strong and it was going to be a long wait for death to, mercifully, claim her. In the meantime, she could not possibly turn her back on her obligations. She had made a vow to William, and vows were sacred. She would not flee with this child whose gentle breathing she could hear across the room and who so idolized her father, for all of his rages.

Sleep had found her, finally, but only as the sun began to rise. Soon afterwards, she woke to the smell of the pancakes William was concocting downstairs, his way of making amends. And when she and Stella stepped into the kitchen, William came over to put his arms around Mrs. Adams. "I don't deserve you," he said. "Such a damn fool." He looked so miserable that once again, her heart warmed to him. *Not just you*, she had thought.

She looked into Simon's face now and saw the torment there. He was trapped in that dark place from where she knew it must seem there was only one way out. Unless you have been flung into that airless dungeon and heard the door clang shut against the light, you could not possibly understand the horror of it.

"I know," she wanted to tell him, but they had never spoken about such things. Their friendship was based on their connection to the other people in their lives. Both Mrs. Adams and Simon were naturally reticent anyway, so discussing other people came far more easily than revealing anything about themselves. She knew from Grace that when Simon had lost his twin brother at fifteen, he had withdrawn to his room and stayed there for a month, speaking to no one. When he finally did come out, he announced that he would not talk about the event nor mention Jeremy's name ever again. As far as she knew he had kept his word. His face reminded Mrs. Adams of her grandfather's as he lay in his coffin at the funeral—a simulation of a human face but there was nobody actually behind the waxen mask, nobody home.

As they sat encapsulated in the wild and perilous night, she began to feel light-headed. "Strange," she said. "I don't believe I've ever seen so much lightning, yet there's not much thunder now."

"It's probably moving off until another cell comes by,"

Simon said. The fallen tree, he noticed, had downed a live power line, which was now arcing on the road too close to the car for comfort. Their safest option was probably to stay put in the ditch until the storm passed, though, if anything, it seemed to him to have intensified. He glanced at Mrs. Adams. Her face, in the flickering light of the sparking wires, looked sickly. "Are you feeling all right?" he asked.

"Bit woozy," she said, and slumped sideways. Simon twisted to reach for her. Awkwardly, he tried to position her so that her head might get some blood flow.

"Oh, silly," she murmured. "Such a *nuisance* ..."

"When was the last time you had something to drink?" Simon asked.

"Cup of decaf," she murmured. She sat back and closed her eyes.

Simon peered out the window. "Water, water, everywhere ..." he said. "You wouldn't have any water in the car, would you?"

"Just Heineken, I'm afraid," she replied.

"Beer!" In all these years, he had never seen his mother-in-law with a beer in her hand.

"For Angelo, the gardener. He won't buy that kind for himself because it's more expensive, so I picked up a case or two for his birthday."

Simon stretched over the seat. "Tell me it's not in the trunk. Ahah!" He pulled a six-pack into the front seat. The next challenge would be opening the bottle.

Mrs. Adams reached into her bag and handed him a Swiss Army knife. "This ought to do it."

"Lily!" he exclaimed. "And I thought I was beyond being surprised by you."

"Amy gave it to me years ago, in my stocking. In case I got marooned on a desert island, I guess, and needed a corkscrew."

"Well, she got the marooned part right," Simon said, prying the top off a bottle. "Here. Drink this."

She took a swallow, grimaced a bit and took another before handing it back to him. "Keep me company, why don't you. The car suddenly lifted, surging forward a few feet. They could hear the water churning outside. "My goodness!" she cried. "What was that?"

"Ditch is flooding," Simon said.

They sat rock still, as if they might prevent catastrophe by not moving. But there was a rumbling beneath them as the waters passed through and they were forced into motion again, this time with the front end of the car left pointed skyward.

"Do you suppose there's more deluge on its way?" Mrs. Adams asked. Her voice trembled.

Simon chose not to answer. He ran his hand along the side of his seat. "I take back every derogatory thing I ever said about this car. I don't believe it's leaking at all." He handed the beer back to Mrs. Adams and opened one for himself. She guzzled at it gratefully until it was half empty. Simon had to smile at the sight of his ladylike mother-in-law knocking back a brew. As always, her silver hair was pulled back into a braided coil at the nape of her neck.

Mrs. Adams heaved a contented sigh, pointed her index finger at Simon's chest and prodded it lightly. "You know," she said, as if a significant and original thought had just occurred to her. "I almost left my husband."

Simon gaped at her. "William?"

She laughed. "Did I misplace another one somewhere? Of course, William. I was just thinking, what a coincidence. You're divorced and I *wanted* to be divorced."

"Lily, are you just a little drunk?" he asked.

"Mm," she answered thoughtfully. "Probably more than a little bit," she said. "Doesn't take much, you know, for a skinny old chicken like me. Quite pleasant, actually." She took another dainty pull from the bottle. "He drank, of course," she said. "Tried to keep it away from Stella and me, but he would come home reeking of it, and after one of those bouts he'd be in a black mood for days. He had a *terrible* temper, lost it all the time."

"I saw a few of those," Simon said. "Once, he broke his golf club. I didn't even know it was possible."

"I was not prepared for a person like William," she said. "In my family, there was nary a raised voice. If my parents were having what they called a 'debate,' they would speak German so my brother and I wouldn't understand. William's house. Like a cage of wild animals. His mother drank too much, his father was always ranting about something at the top of his lungs, and he and William always at loggerheads …."

The wind shook the car as if for emphasis. She ran her hand across her forehead.

"Are you all right, Lily?" Simon asked.

"My," she murmured. "I don't think I've strung so many words together at one time in my entire life. What's gotten into me?"

"A pint of Heineken," Simon said.

"What a boring old toot."

"On the contrary," Simon remarked. "Why *didn't* you divorce him?"

"I suppose I was afraid. Women were so helpless back then, at least women like me. I can count to ten in Arabic. That wasn't exactly going to help me get a job in Indian Wells, and I'd never have taken Stella away from her father. She adored him."

"You certainly didn't let it show," Simon said. "I remember a lot of laughter."

"Oh, hells bells," she said. "Anyway, I suppose he was the love of my life."

Simon laughed, but Lily blinked as if startled by the statement.

"I've never considered myself a romantic," she said. "But there was … certainly, there was … gratitude."

Mrs. Adams closed her eyes. Simon waited quietly, long enough for him to suppose she might have fallen asleep.

"And then, there was Jed." He could barely hear her.

"Jed?"

"The baby. The one who died," she said.

Stella had mentioned something, but it had been just the vaguest fragment of family history, something no one ever spoke about. Again, he waited.

"Stella was three," she continued. We brought Jed home from the hospital but he'd picked something up, some sort of infection." She stopped for another sip of beer.

"Lily, you don't have to …."

She shook her head. "We phoned the doctor in the middle of the night. He was annoyed, thought we were being overly anxious. Anyway, the baby *didn't* improve and by the time we got him to the hospital, it was too late. It was entirely my fault."

"How do you figure that?" Simon asked.

"William wanted to phone again, but Jed didn't seem that sick … and I was, oh, embarrassed, I guess. It went against my grain, to disturb anybody in the middle of the night like that. Stella'd had fevers, too, and she always recovered."

A single tear slid down her cheek. Simon reached for her hand.

"Anyway, he never blamed me, not once."

They listened to the rain for a moment, more of a steady patter now.

"Loss is so particular," she said. "I think of how Jed had a little cowlick at the back of his head, a little Iroquois feather that stuck straight up …." She pointed to a spot below her left breast. "There's a bruise here that's never going away, as long as I live."

Simon kissed her hand and replaced it on her lap.

"The thing is," she said, "your relationship with somebody doesn't stop changing just because one of you died."

They both sat staring out at the blackness and odd flickering light. After a while, Simon made a noise like a cough.

"Jeremy was pigeon-toed," he said. The words came out half strangled.

Mrs. Adams felt the world come to a dead halt. She sucked in her breath.

"He toed in," Simon pushed on. "Jeremy did."

"Oh, my dear," Mrs. Adams said. She felt reverent, a witness to some sacred dawning.

Simon leaned forward, bracing his head against the steering wheel. "It made him self-conscious," Simon said, so softly that Mrs. Adams had to strain to hear him.

"He had this muscular build he was so proud of," Simon

went on, "but his feet, he thought they made him look ridiculous. He used to practice walking but of course it didn't work, though maybe over time ... well, he'd be forty-seven now, like me."

Grace Vanderwall had told Mrs. Adams about Jeremy's death, the cruelty of it as he slipped down into the bog on the moors, about Simon's futile attempts to save him. It had taken two days of complicated digging to retrieve the boy's body.

Mrs. Adams stroked his back. It felt steamy, the way Stella's had when she cried her heart out—Simon, now, like a little boy beside her. He sat up and stared into the black night.

"All right, dear?" Mrs. Adams asked.

He looked at her as if he didn't know who she was. She watched his face slowly regain the present. "Where in the hell did that come from?" he said. "I'm sorry, Lily."

"Well, no," she said. She wanted in the worst way to pet him, to run her fingers through his damp hair.

"I'm stuck in the mud, Lily," Simon said.

"Why, yes," Mrs. Adams said. "We're well and truly mired."

"No. On the moors, I meant, with Jeremy."

Mrs. Adams laid her hand against his cheek. "Ah," she said.

And there they sat, holding hands and waiting for rescue, which came at last as morning broke over the exhausted, resilient old forest.

THE LIST

Once every month or so, Lily and Stella alternated visiting one another. When it was Lily's turn, she would get on the train and take the trip down to Hudson. This time, in a gesture of independence, she had forbidden Stella to pick her up at the train station, so Stella paced at the front gate until she saw the cab headed up the street.

"Woo hoo!" Lily called, leaning her head out the window, fluttering her hand like a white handkerchief.

Stella paid the driver and helped Lily out of the taxi. "You know you don't *have* to come down here, Ma," Stella said. "I'm perfectly happy to drive up to see you." She reached for the vintage '60s purse that served as Lily's suitcase. She always traveled light, a practice that she had passed along to Stella, certainly a boon for international globe-trotting. Lily simply brought along a nightgown, an extra sweater and a toothbrush. And, of course, a good detective story. As for underwear, she simply washed it out each night in the bathroom sink. Somehow she always managed to look well put together, like today in a denim skirt, a thick cable cardigan and low heels. Stella had never seen Lily in a pair of sneakers or slacks in her entire life.

Lily tucked a twenty-dollar bill into Stella's pocket for the cab fare. Having learned that there was no point in trying to refuse it, Stella simply held out her arm for her mother to hang onto.

"Good for me to have an outing," Lily said. "I wish you could have seen the rivers out the window. The canals, too. They made the whole world watery, like a French painting."

But Stella didn't answer. She was trying to adjust to the fact that her mother had somehow shrunk since her last visit. They had been the same height when Stella was growing up; now Lily barely reached Stella's ear. Stella felt a sudden cold breath against the back of her neck and shivered.

"Look at that," Lily said. "Your tulips are much further along than ours."

Stella covered her mother's hand with her own. "Come in. You're freezing. Those tulips will be there all weekend." She tugged gently at her mother, shaking off the vague sense of foreboding and held the door open.

"I don't mind the bus," Lily said. "Although I have to say it's a waste of money buying a ticket when I could be driving."

"Don't start, Ma," Stella said.

"It's just foolish, that's all. I have plenty of good driving years ahead of me. Now I have to hire a taxi to do my grocery shopping or get a haircut half a mile up the road."

Stella opted not to engage. It had been a nightmare getting rid of that old monster car. Lily had driven it into a snowdrift that winter on her way to the post office. Then, as if that hadn't been enough warning, Stella got a phone call from Fritz Jenovyk, her mother's state trooper friend. He'd begun tailing Lily. Her driving was erratic to say the least, and he was afraid she'd kill herself or somebody else.

"She drives through town at sixty, and not always on her side of the road," Fritz said. "I've pulled her over for speeding a couple of times, but I really just can't bring myself to give her a ticket. That's not going to help anything."

"Are you saying she needs to give up her license?" Stella had asked.

"Afraid so," Fritz said. "And soon."

There had been a lot of resistance. Lily continued to drive until finally Fritz was forced to take away her keys.

"She almost cried," Fritz had reported, heartbroken himself.

At this point there were merely the occasional mild complaints from Lily, mainly because they were expected.

Recently she had even told Stella that it was a relief to be driven around town "like the Queen of the May."

"What do you think, Ma?" Stella asked. "Isn't it about time for a little colored water?"

Lily glanced at her watch. Actually, it was William's watch with the gold band. Lily had worn it every day since his death, a habit that Stella found touching.

"Without a doubt," Lily said. "I'll just go up and settle in."

"Let me know if you need anything," Stella said.

"What was that, dear?" Lily asked from the second stair. "You need to speak up."

"Holler, I said, if you need anything." If her mother was getting deaf, this was the first time Stella had been made aware of it. She watched her mother climb the stairs, deliberately and with a firm grip on the banister. She's going to leave me, Stella thought to herself.

It was a cool May evening, but the cushions on the porch swing out back were still warm with sunshine. Stella brought out their drinks and some Goldfish on a tray. Lily drank bourbon, one part bourbon to ten parts water, from a bottle that had been in the liquor closet since 1979. When Stella sat down, Lily snuggled right up next to her. Lily had never been much of a hugger, as she put it. But lately, after a lifetime of arm's length affection, Lily had finally relaxed into the comfort of physical contact with her daughter.

Stella held the crackers out. "I want you to eat every last one of these, Ma. I can feel your bones through your sweater."

"I'm a shrinker, that's all," Lily said. She selected a single Goldfish that sat in her palm for several moments, stranded, as if on a riverbank. "That's what happens when a person gets older. Remember your Aunt Maude? Now there was a sweller. She was so enormous that they had to put her in a special box and haul her to the cemetery in a pickup truck."

Stella laughed and felt herself begin to unwind. There had been a garden swing back at the old house in Indian Wells. Stella had been such a hyperactive child, one leg always pumping, fingers tapping nonstop. She was often aggravated, often with her mother in particular. When she sat in the swing, though, she was able to calm herself. It was one of the first things she and Simon had installed at the Hudson house.

Stella inhaled the scent of new growth in the garden and closed her eyes. She was so enjoying the proximity of her mother. It seemed inconceivable that there could ever have been tension between them.

"Now, tell me everything," Lily said.

"Haven't heard a peep," Stella answered. Any conversation between them always began with Amy and her doings. "Have you?"

"I had a postcard with Grand Central Station on it. It reminded me of when I first took her there, you remember? She looked up at the ceiling and said, 'Big *church*.'" They sipped their drinks, savoring the memory. "I wish she would find a nice man," Lily said, "but I probably sound like a broken record."

"Yeah, well, nice men aren't exactly falling from trees," Stella remarked.

Lily peered at her. "Hm ..." she said. Stella had forbidden Lily to harass her about her social life, but there was an epic novel within that one drawn-out syllable.

Stella took a generous sip of wine. "I remember when you taught me how to make hollyhock dolls," she said.

"Yes, and then you taught Amy."

They sat for a moment, watching a pair of rabbits nibble at the new shoots in the very back of the garden. The shadows were lengthening across the lawn. Stella often looked back on her childhood years as being fraught with turmoil. It was pleasant to remember the happy times sitting in the yard with her mother, playing with the flowers. She reached for Lily's hand.

"Why was I always blowing up at you when I was a kid, Ma?" Stella asked. "I can't recall a single reason for it, just that I was always mad."

Lily smiled. "The same reason Amy was mad at you, I expect. I was your mother."

Stella thought about that for a moment. "I couldn't even say 'good morning' to Amy without her cringing," she said. "In fact, she's still a pretty accomplished eye roller."

Stella set another Goldfish onto Lily's palm. "What about your mother?" Stella had never met her. She had died of malaria before Stella was born.

"I took a train ride with her one time in Egypt," Lily said. "I must have been about twelve. She fell asleep next to me and pretty soon her head fell back against the seat. I'll never forget—her mouth gaped open like a horrid big fish and she began to snore. It was so mortifying. If I could only have moved to another car, or another country. Or just died."

Stella laughed, but then there was that chilling sensation like a cold finger drawn up her spine. Stella's grandmother on that train had, in all likelihood, been younger than she, Stella, was this very moment. Now she was dead, and that girl Lily, herself, was an old woman. Seventy-seven was old, no getting around it, and there would come a time, sooner rather than later … Stella felt her eyes begin to mist. When had her mother developed that tremor in her hands?

They sat sipping their drinks for a while, swimming amongst the flotsam and jetsam of other decades. Then Stella shook herself free of the past. Lily had finally consumed the Goldfish, she noticed. "Okay, Ma," she said. "Let's go pump some vittles into you."

They sat at the table indulging in their favorite comfort foods—Lily with macaroni and cheese, Stella with nachos. The conversation now revolved around movies. When Stella was in grade school, Lily would keep her home whenever something exceptional happened to be playing in the movie theater, Lily's definition of exceptional being anything that had a gangster in it. If organized crime wasn't available, cowboys would do nicely. *High Noon* was so gripping that they sat and watched it twice. Then Lily would give Stella a note for her teacher the next day, "Stella was indisposed," it would say. It wasn't a lie, Lily had explained. Stella was indisposed to go to *school*, that was all.

"I think *The Red River*'s on tonight," Stella said, reluctantly scooping up the last tortilla chip.

"You know, dear," Lily said, "I'm afraid I'm just an old poop. Much as I would adore watching the bewitching Mr. Clift, I believe I'll just head on up to bed."

It was around midnight when Lily came downstairs, one of Amy's old winter coats tossed over her nightgown for warmth. Stella had fallen asleep by the television.

"Wake up, Stella," Lily said, standing over her.

Stella shifted a little, blinked and looked at Lily as if she'd just stepped out of a dream. Her mother was holding a manila envelope, which she shook in front of Stella's face. "I'll make you some coffee if you like, but you're going to wake up."

Stella squinted at the envelope. "What've you got there, Ma?" she asked, sitting up with a yawn.

"Something I found in the wastebasket by your desk."

"What on earth were you doing, poking through my stuff?" Stella was waking up now, and fast. "Give it here."

Lily held it away. "You didn't open it," she said. "Why?"

"Maybe because it's from Simon and I don't need any more grief."

"All right, I can see that. But don't you think it's telling that it's been sitting in that waste basket for over two weeks?" Lily asked. "What's the message there?"

"Probably that I'm a lousy housekeeper."

"You have to read this," Lily said.

"No, I don't," Stella said. "And you neither."

"I already have," Lily said.

"You read my *mail?*" Stella asked, incredulous. "I could have you arrested." She stood up now and grabbed the envelope from her mother.

"While I'm awaiting the constabulary," Lily said, "you're going to sit down with those pages."

"Absolutely not."

"Don't be a coward, Stella. It's unlike you."

Stella stared back at Lily, seized by a mixture of rage and

disbelief that left her uncharacteristically tongue-tied.

Lily took a breath and spoke quietly. "You're my brave girl, Stella. You've faced rampaging elephants. You can certainly read a letter from your ex-husband."

"Yeah, well, Mother, elephants don't have the clout to break my heart into smithereens," Stella said.

"I've always been so proud of you," Lily said. "Don't let me down now."

"Proud of me?" Stella retorted. "You know, it might have been nice if you'd told me that, just once." She got off the couch and began to pace back and forth in front of the empty fireplace.

"You're right," Lily said. "I should have and I'm sorry. I suppose I was terrified by your job, by the danger. Maybe because I had lost one child, I was overly frightened that I would lose you. The last thing I would have wanted was to say anything that would encourage you."

Stella stared at Lily in disbelief. Revelations were pouring from her mother's mouth faster than she could possibly take them in. She raised her hands. "All right, all right," she said. "Let's just calm down, okay? The issue here is the envelope. It's my property, and you had no right to open it, much less read the contents."

"Oh, Stella …" Lily said, shaking her head. In the old days, she would have been afraid that Stella would be about to have an episode, but Lily had moved past that. Simon had taught her how. And the fact that Stella was now holding the envelope defiantly to her chest Lily took to be a good sign. "I'm cold and I'm tired," she said, "so I'm going up to bed. Just read it, Stella. Read the damn thing."

She turned and walked out of the room. Stella heard her slow tread on the stairs.

Stella sat there for some time with the pages in her lap. After a while, she got up to make a fire and pour herself a glass of wine. She sipped at it thoughtfully while the logs flared up, then settled into a crackling blaze.

Finally, she picked up the first page and glanced at it sideways as she might have done while watching a scary movie.

"For my darling Stella," the letter began.

Damn him, Stella thought, vowing to read no further. But just at that moment, a cinder exploded with a loud pop. Surely that was a sign that she ought to at least try.

It was a list, she saw, with sentences in capital letters. Simon had always loved lists. With Stella often traveling and Amy in school, he was in charge of running the household. Stella had loved the reminders he left on the refrigerator door, many of them executed in rhyme schemes: *If you're looking for ways to improve your demeanor/ Please pick up your skirt from our friendly dry cleaner.* The receipt would be attached. Or, for Amy: *Before you go out, could you please wash the dishes/ And after, remember to feed both the fishes.*

"I am hoping that you can bring yourself to read this," Simon had written at the top of this new list so many years later. "But no response is required or expected. xxS."

> "HEREWITH AN INCOMPLETE LISTING OF THE REASONS THAT I LOVE STELLA MEREDITH ADAMS VANDERWALL AND ALWAYS WILL:
> "BECAUSE OF YOUR DEDICATION TO YOUR WORK, E.G., THE TRUCK."

Stella regarded her Peace Corps years the way other people did their college experience. Listening to her friends talk about the anti-Vietnam War protests as if they had been some kind of national fraternity party, she was silent. It was just that her coming-of-age had been so fundamentally different, her plunge into the reality of African poverty a world away from the beer blasts and all-night cram sessions, the protests and the sit-ins.

Her village in the Ivory Coast boasted a single vehicle, a beat-up yellow '64 Citroen 2CV Fourgo, affectionately known as "Le Coeur," for "Coeur de Lion." A "gift" to the village from the secretaire général of the district, whose wife had managed to strip all the gears except reverse, it now sat in the center of town for months on end, and was used mainly as a playground for the children. Stella had been coached in minimal auto repair skills, but nothing she administered could persuade Le Coeur to move in a forward direction. One day, Moussa, the Gaullist who lived next door in a bamboo frame mud-covered house like Stella's, cut his leg with a machete. He bled without ceasing and Stella realized she had to get him to the nearest village with a doctor. But how? she wondered as she stared helplessly at the truck. While others might well succumb to kicking the tires in frustration, Stella characteristically chose to encourage rather than criticize.

"Come on, now, Braveheart, you can do this," Stella urged the vehicle, loading Moussa into the truck. "You can do this." She backed onto the "main road," a single rutted lane. The rearview mirror had been snapped off long ago, so she was forced to open her door and lean out to see where she was going, the kicked-up dust clinging to the sweat dripping from her face. That backwards nine-mile trip saved Moussa from bleeding to death. Not that Stella spent any time congratulating herself for it. The next day, she found a mechanic who, in exchange for her high school ring, managed to retrieve a single, temperamental forward gear for Le Coeur.

The experience was the first of so many that propelled Stella into a life of service, though she might not have thought of it that way, let alone talked about it. She was shy about expressing her feelings regarding her job, imagining that they might sound hollow or pompous to anyone else. With Simon, though, she shared them: that she was one of the privileged people who get to see firsthand a positive impact on some other human being; that it horrified her to think she had come so close to foregoing the Peace Corps for business school instead; that her work enriched her, fed her, buoyed her. Simon understood it all, never once chastising her for taking off for some tangled jungle even as the dishwasher was flooding the kitchen or the dog needed surgery.

"BECAUSE I CAME HOME FROM WORK ONE SUMMER DAY AND FOUND YOU SPRAWLED FACEDOWN ON THE FRONT LAWN."

Stella had been inhaling the earth. Sometimes the scent was simply too intoxicating to ignore. Stella felt a smile prickling at the corners of her mouth and caught herself. It was the wine, that's all. She would not do him the favor of reacting. She would skim through as if prancing delicately across the surface of a treacherous spider web.

"BECAUSE YOU LOVE OUR DAUGHTER EXTRAVAGANTLY."

"WHEN AMY HAD JUST GOTTEN HER DRIVER'S PERMIT SHE RAN OVER A BIRD. I CAME HOME TO FIND YOU BOTH ON AMY'S BED. SHE WAS SITTING AT THE EDGE AND YOU WERE BEHIND HER WITH YOUR LEGS AND ARMS WRAPPED AROUND HER, ROCKING HER AS SHE WEPT. I'LL NEVER FORGET THE LOOK ON YOUR FACE AS YOU HELD HER."

Stella had forgotten the incident about the starling, how Amy had fretted that it was merely half dead, lying there suffering, awaiting another crushing blow from an oncoming vehicle. Stella had phoned the local wildlife center, eliciting a promise that someone would go out to the site and dispatch the animal.

What Stella was inclined to remember were the times she had let Amy down. There weren't many, but still. Exhausted already, Stella sighed and picked up the pages again.

"BECAUSE OF YOUR 2:00 A.M. WEATHER REPORTS."

Stella had always been a sleepwalker, even as a child when she would let herself out of the house in the summertime and wander around the yard barefoot amid a cloud of fireflies. But a few months after Stella and Simon had moved in together, he told her over breakfast that she had awakened him in the night.

"Quick!" she had called. "Come and see! It's snowing!" At first, he had thought groggily that there must be a storm outside, but then he realized that Stella was not at the window but was in fact standing with her back to him, staring into the closet.

"Oh, it's so pretty," she went on. "I love it when it drifts."

He had taken her gently by the shoulders and ushered her back into bed. She had stared up at him with brilliant vacant eyes. "Go to sleep, Stella," he had said. "It's time for sleep."

Six months later, she woke him again. She stood beside the bed in her raincoat holding an umbrella. "It's time to go," she had told him. "Here," she said, handing him the umbrella. "It's pouring."

Simon spoke quietly so as not to startle her awake. "All right, Stella," he said, taking the umbrella. "Let's get you in out of the rain."

"Is it time to go home?" she asked.

"Yes, sweetheart," Simon said, and put her back to bed.

The nocturnal weather reports came in cycles, often showing up a week or so after a trip when Stella's attempts to adjust to American time were not facilitated by the malaria vaccine that was still messing with her dreams. Ever since the divorce, Stella sometimes found a random sweater beside her bed in the morning, or a stray pair of shoes, and gathered that she must have been on an adventure during the night.

Stella set the pages beside her on the couch and stood up. She had been sitting with one leg bent under her and it had fallen asleep. She picked up her wine glass and paced back and forth to get her circulation moving again. If only the numbness in her leg would travel up to her brain, which was functioning all too keenly.

"BECAUSE OF THE WAY YOU LOOK AFTER WE MAKE LOVE—LIKE YOU'RE NOT QUITE SURE WHERE YOU ARE, ALL DAZED AND LIMP AND BEAUTIFUL."

Stella realized now that she would not stop reading until she'd finished every page. Were she was told that the world was about to end, she would keep on reading. Especially then.

"BECAUSE YOU DEMONSTRATE EQUAL CAPACITY FOR ATHLETIC GRACE AND FOR EXTREME KLUTZINESS … SOMETIMES ON THE SAME OCCASION."

Stella was always sporting a bruise or a scrape from some mishap or other. The example that popped into her head now was the one she earned on that women's bike race in the Catskills.

She had used her customary tactic of biding her time, allowing the younger cyclists to exhaust themselves on the early calf-punishing inclines. During the last quarter hour of the twenty-mile course, she pulled out all the stops and slid easily past the finish line, alone. Simon and Amy were waiting for her, cheering and waving balloons. She pumped her fists in the air at them and then, just as the race organizer was approaching to place the winner's ribbon around her neck, she shifted her weight awkwardly to topple over and break her foot. She had been in a cast for twelve weeks.

On the rare occasion that she and Simon attended a formal event, Stella would step into her most glamorous cocktail dress—the black one that showed off her slender body—and there, inevitably, on one leg or the other, would be some spectacular wound.

"Jesus, Stella, how did you get that?" Simon would ask.

"I don't know," she would say.

"Don't you want to put a Band-Aid on it?"

"Nah," she would reply. "Better to let it breathe." And off they would go.

"BECAUSE OF THE TENDERNESS IN YOUR HANDS AS YOU STAND BEHIND YOUR MOTHER, BRAIDING HER HAIR, YOUR CONFIDENCES AND REMINISCENCES ENTWINING TOGETHER AS ARTFULLY AS THOSE SHINING SILVER STRANDS."

She thought of the old heart asleep upstairs and felt a lump swell in her throat. This vacillation between comedy and poignancy had her reeling. Even planted firmly in the corner of the couch, she felt she was falling, falling, into a dangerous place. She took several deep breaths and glanced at the remaining pages. Not far to go now. Surely she could summon the nerve to finish. She picked up the next one.

"BECAUSE YOU ARE THE ONLY PERSON I EVER HEARD OF WHO GOT FIRED BY THEIR DENTIST."

Doctor Pascal had asked her if she would consider closing her eyes while he worked on her. When she asked why, he explained that her staring directly into his face the entire time was unnerving. He had beautiful eyes, though, like stained-glass chips of brown and green; and besides, what else was there to look at? She had tried, but failed, and the next time she called for an appointment, his secretary had referred her to someone else.

"BECAUSE OF THE BATHTUB."

With instant recognition, Stella recalled their third anniversary, which they celebrated on a hot August weekend at an upscale bed-and-breakfast out on the north fork of Long Island. She had been in Africa for almost a month, so on Friday night after an early meal in the dining room, they hurried upstairs. There was a charming claw-foot tub in their bathroom, which Stella suggested they share. She turned on the spigots and returned to the bedroom to find Simon stripped to the waist, lean and muscular. Overwhelmed with desire, Stella had propelled him onto the bed and then they were lost to the world.

Suddenly, there was a pounding on the door, accompanied by frenzied shouts. Stella grabbed her robe and went to investigate. The manager shouldered past her and headed straight for the bathroom.

"Wait," she said, but even in that moment, she understood. She stared at Simon who, already there, had his hands to his head. In the bathroom, Stella's flip-flops were afloat on an inch of water covering the entire floor, fed by the cascade from the overflowing tub.

They had thrown themselves on the mercy of the manager, pledging to pay for repairs and apologizing repeatedly. It was worse than it seemed, though. Not only had the flood seeped through to the dining room below, but it had dripped onto the ceiling fan which proceeded to fling water all around the room, drenching every person there.

"It rained on *everybody!*" the manager shouted.

Alas, this information regarding the fan was challenging Stella's composure. She had glanced at Simon, a mistake.

"Wow," he breathed softly, with profound and totally inappropriate pride.

Stella, undone, let out a strangled hoot, which she proceeded to mask with a coughing fit as she dove for the nearest door—of a closet, as it turned out, into which she withdrew in paroxysms of hilarity.

Even now, she laughed. What a gift, she thought, to have this memory back. And so she read it again.

"YOU NEVER MINDED MY CAREER."

It had taken a while for Simon to figure out that he needn't be a businessman like his father or a journalist like his mother. He began showing houses at the suggestion of a friend. To his great surprise, he had loved it. Stella found it heartwarming that he so enjoyed helping people find a home. She looked forward to his descriptions of the cast of characters, both buyers and sellers, with their dramas, not to mention the houses themselves, and how revealing they were about those inhabiting them. Sometimes, when meeting new people, Stella had seen the conversation die when Simon answered the inevitable question of what he did for a living. Detecting often the edge of inadvertent condescension towards him, she would blaze up protectively. But somehow Simon didn't mind and told her she shouldn't either.

Stella saw that she was at the end now. She picked up the last page reluctantly, aware that this slender thread of words connecting her to Simon would, in a matter of moments, snap. She read the words slowly, reverently.

"AND FINALLY, MY DARLING, BECAUSE YOU DID NOT BULLY ME ABOUT JEREMY. I WOULD TALK WITH YOU ABOUT HIM NOW, ABOUT HOW I RESURRECTED HIM OVER THESE PAST MONTHS ONLY TO BURY HIM AGAIN, ONCE AND FOR ALL. ABOUT HOW HE NO LONGER STANDS BETWEEN ME AND THE WORLD. ABOUT HOW I AM NOW FREE TO REMEMBER HIM AND HONOR HIM AND HOW I AM NOW, AT LAST, FREE TO LOVE YOU, AND AMY, WHICH I DO WITH ALL MY HEART."

.   .   .

Stella curled herself into a ball in the corner of the couch and covered her face with her hands. She had no idea how long she was there, nor even what precisely she was thinking, only that she was exhausted by the time she came to. Feeling Lily's hand on her shoulder, Stella looked up, took her mother's hand, and held it in both of hers.

"Did I make a mistake forcing this on you?" Lily asked.

Stella shook her head, rose from the couch and headed for the front hall.

"You're going out now?" Lily asked. "It's one o'clock in the morning."

"Yes," Stella said. "I'm going out."

"At least put on a jacket!" Lily called after her. But the front door had already clicked shut.

INSIDE OUT

Amy: 1994

It was two years to the day since Amy's grandmother died. Stella and Simon had worried about leaving Amy alone on the painful anniversary, but in fact it was her parents' concern that weighed on her most. Amy had planned her own personal memorial, and it did not include anyone else. So last night she had had an early dinner at her childhood home in Hudson, after which a car service arrived to pick up her parents.

"Sure you'll be okay, puddlesplash?" her father asked, his pet names meteorological of late. Earlier in the day she had been "blue skies."

"Uhh!" Amy responded through the crush of Stella's bruising hug.

The taxi honked outside, and at last her parents set off for JFK. They would catch a flight for London in the morning and make the drive to Devon where her father had grown up.

Amy slept in her old bed in her old room and woke early, conscious that she had been busy with dreams in the night. Her head was filled with images that tumbled around like clothes in a dryer. She lay quiet for an hour or so, making the transition to reality, but before long, she was on her way to the town of Indian Wells on an unusually warm spring morning. She drove straight to the cemetery. It occupied a gentle hill on the fringe of the local golf course about half a mile from her grandparents' house, now occupied by a fashionable young couple who had painted the entire interior in an array of whites, including the original eighteenth century pine floors.

Inching her car up the pitted access road, Amy remembered the countless times she had tagged along with her grandfather as he played the course. The distinction of being his "caddy" had made her feel very grown up. He would ask her what club he should use, giving her a thumbs-up if she got it right, and explaining why if she guessed wrong. She parked now at the fifth hole, which abutted the graveyard. It was a challenging hole, very short—you wouldn't go lower than a five iron. But the green sat on top of a steep hill, like a traffic cone with its head lopped off. Every single time she and her grandfather had played it, he would stop before teeing off and say, "My gravestone's going to be *right* there …." He would point with his club. "But if I don't make a hole in one on this son of a bitch before I die, bury me someplace else. I don't want to have to look at the goddamn thing for eternity."

"Grandad!" Amy would chastise him. "You're not going to die!" But in the end he shot not one, but two holes in one before the fatal heart attack and wound up with a first-class view.

She got out of the car and opened the trunk, removing a tarpaulin and a carton. She walked them through a break in the hedge and stood for a moment, gazing at the neat rows of graves where she and her friends had spent so many hours during the long summer days, playing hide and seek and inventing treasure hunts. There was an intoxicating smell of recently cut grass. Clusters of daffodils caught the morning sun.

Amy spread the tarpaulin out between her grandparents' headstones, noting that her grandfather's, more than fifteen years old now, could use some attention. She stared at the inscriptions on first his and then her grandmother's. She accepted the fact of her grandfather's demise now, though for a while it had seemed impossible that such a force could be so unexpectedly cut down. But her grandmother was an entirely different story; even as a child Amy could be brought to tears merely by imagining Gran's inevitable departure. Now that the first two years of heartache were past, Amy had work to do, and she planned to complete it today.

Installing herself cross-legged on the tarpaulin, she removed a hardcover book from the carton: *The Children's Eyes,* a novel by Amy Vanderwall. She stared at the cover, a misty photograph of a pair of lovers in a leafy wood. It was beautiful. She wished Gran had seen it in its final incarnation.

A writer friend had warned her that the appearance of your just-published book in a bookstore window was apt to be somewhat of a letdown. How wrong he was! It was embarrassing how many hours she had loitered in front of various bookstores throughout New York, gazing at her novel and fully understanding what it meant to swell with pride. It was like being pumped full of a giddy gas that lifted you straight off the pavement to bob deliriously around among the skyscrapers.

She set the book down and peered into the carton, which was crammed with letters, hers and Gran's. It turned out that they had both been storing them away over the years, so that now there was a comprehensive collection of their correspondence. Amy had pulled a selection from both Gran's and her own that seemed particularly appropriate for her intentions on this day. She began with an early letter, its disciplined sentences on Gran's awful blue stationery that she bought each year from the mentally challenged son of a neighbor. She always ordered too much, which accounted for the dozen boxes in her closet when she died. The familiarity of it, the tactile reality, seemed cruel. This was what was left of Gran's voice, these flimsy bits of paper? Amy held the letter to her chest.

"Gran," she whispered, and felt her eyes prick.

She sat for some moments, calming herself, but soon she became aware that the words in the box beside her were practically jumping off the pages, rattling and rustling and demanding attention. She had come here, after all, to read and to celebrate. There was a rite to complete as well, but that could wait awhile.

As on most of her letters, Gran had penciled at the top a number representing Amy's age at the time.

8
Dear Gran,

How is Lord Stingwell? Do you think that there is a

Lady Stingwell?
Love, Amy

Lord Stingwell, Amy remembered, was a wasp who had bored a hole into an eave of Gran's house. She and Amy had spent an entire hour sipping lemonade and watching the hardworking creature stuff pieces of leaf and straw into his new home. Gran had remarked that he ought to be knighted for his "enterprise and tenacity," two words that Amy readily added to her list of favorites. Her grandmother could always be counted on for a fresh supply.

Gran had replied:

Dearest Amy,
Lord Stingwell has indeed been seen about town with a winsome lady friend. I hesitate to elevate her to the status of nobility if only because her clothing leaves much to be desired. Her dress is drab. Her antennae droop. Well, you'll see for yourself next weekend. Shall we cook something?
Love, Gran

Amy set the letter down and sailed off on a memory voyage back into the big kitchen at Indian Creek where she had spent so much time with her grandmother. Some of their concoctions became classics in the family lore—for instance, the peanut butter ice cream that yanked a filling out of William Adams' bicuspid. Nonetheless, the two persevered. Mostly what they did was laugh.

9

Dear Gran,
Somebody pulled the vine down in Kramer's Woods! It was the best vine by *far* for swinging. Why would anybody do that? It made me cry so much my face hurt. It was just lying there in the leaves like a great big dead snake.
Love, Amy

What Amy remembered about that incident, along with her outrage, was that the arrangement of words in her letter had mattered. She had struggled over it, trying to work out a way to express to Gran precisely what she meant. The first version had led off with the final sentence. Ultimately, she realized, without quite knowing why exactly, that the dead snake would have more of an impact if she left it for the very end. Funny that all this time later she'd recall that struggle with the language when she couldn't begin to remember who had actually been with her in the woods that day.

> Dearest Amy,
>
> Sometimes it's very hard to understand why people do things. The person who pulled down the vine may have done it very casually, not even thinking about the consequences. Or maybe he didn't even know what it was used for. Or it could be that he did it to be mean. Sadly, there are some in this world who like to destroy. I believe that they are very unhappy with a big empty place inside themselves that, no matter what, they can never fill. I'm sorry that you lost your vine. Maybe you and your friends should have a little ceremony for it, like you did for Anabel's turtle.
>
> Love,
> Gran

The next was also from Gran. Now and then, she or Amy would dash off a random thought and post it to the other before it slipped away.

> Amy dearest,
>
> You had mentioned your lack of interest in sports, despite your athletic abilities. It's not hard to understand. For you, *words* were and are the thing. You eat them. You gobble them up. You get lost in the dictionary as if you were at Tiffany's gazing at jewels. But I agree with your mother, that you need a balance to stay healthy. I'm certain that you can come to an agreement that will satisfy you both.
>
> XO Gran

Amy could almost hear her grandmother's voice in the words as she read them. She strained to hear it, longed to hear it, but it just eluded her. She was beginning to feel an ache in her chest like a bruised rib. Suddenly, a raucous cackling noise above Amy's head caught her attention. She looked up and saw a squirrel perched on a nearby limb. It seemed to be lecturing her.

"Excuse me?" she said out loud.

It leapt from branch to branch, then scurried down the trunk, head first. It halted and settled back on its hind feet to study her.

"You know what?" Amy said, laying her hand against the spot that ached. "This sucks."

She had hoped that reading the correspondence might be healing. What was all that bullshit people spouted about memories being a comfort? About as consoling as a poke in the eye as far as Amy was concerned. What she craved was the tangible fact of her grandmother, sitting beside her on the tarp, with the dappled light playing off her aged face.

"Oh, hell," Amy murmured to herself. This is what she got for having a best friend nearly sixty years her senior. Just then she saw the number at the top of the next letter and experienced a moment of clarity. The year was 1975, a year in which several memorable events had occurred, all of which Amy had ascribed to her having achieved, at last, the double digits; Ron had kissed her in the science lab, most notably. She still remembered the surprise of his teeth against her upper lip.

10

Dear Gran,

I'm feeling much better. I forgot what it was like to be sick and hear the visiting nurse drive up. You just know you're going to get a shot. Also I'm sad that I missed the most amazing week ever. There was a foot of snow on the ground, then it rained so the top layer melted a little. Then it got really cold and the whole world froze so you could ice skate on your yard, or the golf course or anywhere. It was one gigantic rink out there and I had to watch it from my bedroom window. Unfair!

Are you taking care of your cough?

Love,

Amy

Gran had drawn a red star on the top right-hand corner of the next, with a date: "8/89." 1989, the year Amy had finally set her first novel aside and spent a summer agonizing over the prospect of never writing again. And then ... what was that magic, when the idea strikes like a fish surfacing, freed from the depths below to shower beads of water that glisten in the sun?

24

Dear Gran,

I have the first sentence of my new book:

"Ellen O'Malley ... yes, that Ellen O'Malley ... climbed out of the boat and onto the rickety dock in her Fifth Avenue shoes."

Love, Amy

And the reply:

Dearest Amy,

Thank you.

Love, Gran

Leave it to Gran, Amy thought, to respond to such a profoundly personal communication with just those six perfect words. Even praise—*How intriguing, I can't wait to read it*—would have felt like pressure. How did Gran know these things?

Here was a postcard from that period, with the Empire State Building on it. Amy flipped it over and read her own printing in bold letters:

25

GRAN, I GOT FIRED! IMAGINE THAT! XOXO

"Tell me!" Gran had written back, on that ancient lurid stationery.

To which Amy had responded:

I guess I'm just not cut out to be a waitress. I got the orders mixed up last night and gave a man who was allergic to onions a contaminated soup. You wouldn't have believed how much he vomited. Gran, if it hadn't been so tragic, it would have been kind of fascinating in a "Ripley's Believe It Or Not" kind of way. It just went on and on.

So I got canned. And no, Gran, please don't start in about money. I'm fine, I really am. I just need to find some other line of work.

Love, Amy

Gran was always trying to fund her so that she could continue writing without having to work days. But Amy, for her part, worried that her grandmother would run out of money. What if she needed to go into a nursing home one day, or to hire help? The two had reached an unspoken truce in that Gran would give Amy one extravagant check at Christmas and then another at her birthday, which was conveniently five months later.

It had been such an odd sojourn in Amy's life, living in the city. She had felt from her arrival that she was an alien in New York. One day, she had seen a man crossing Madison Avenue with flippers on his feet. The sight was bizarre enough, but even more striking was the fact that nobody else seemed to notice. To Amy, the flipper man seemed like a kindred soul. Of course, it didn't help that she was making precisely zero progress as a published writer.

25

So, dearest Gran, another rejection for the book. That makes eight. I suppose it's possible that if I had an agent there might be more interest, but I haven't had any luck there either. It's the slush pile for me. God knows if anybody ever really reads those manuscripts or if they just send out the turndown letters willy-nilly.

Mom and Dad are pressuring me to give the writing a break (i.e., quit). They think it's too tough on my self-esteem—I should leave New York and come back to Hudson. Dad thinks I could get a job with *The Reporter*, a.k.a. *The Distorter*. I suppose that's writing, too, but I want to make things up, not record the dreary facts.

Do you think I've made a religion out of writing? I'm not sure I believe in God, but I surely do believe in Words.

Love, Amy

Dearest Amy,

Yes, words are important—holy, even, or they can be. A perfect sentence is a contribution to the world. Not everyone can conjure up such a fantastical thing, but *you* can, with your own special voice and your own special light. Whether it's recognized or not, your book is worthy. And so, you must write another, and another after that. If there comes a time—never, I hope, and believe—when you are no longer sustained by your work, that's when you set it aside. And even should that come to pass, you will have enriched the hearts and minds of those who were fortunate enough to read your Words, in whatever form.

With much love and faith,

Gran

25

Dear Gran,

Somebody out there must have read your wonderful letter! I got a great rejection today! It says: "We are sorry that UP RIVER does not fit into our publishing schedule. We would be pleased, however, to read any future material you wish to send along to us. If would be helpful if you would attach a copy of this letter to any submissions. Very truly yours, Ramsey Smith."

I love Ramsey Smith! I adore Ramsey Smith!

I was so inspired that I hopped on the subway and spent a whole afternoon walking on the beach. Listen to this. Suddenly, when I had walked, I don't know, halfway to Montauk, I got this great idea for a final scene, complete with last line of the whole shebang, which is, of course, insanely crucial. But I didn't have anything to write with and I was scared to death I was going to forget it, which is tragic when it happens because you never get it back and what you wind up with isn't anywhere near as good as the initial thought. I had a receipt from the cleaners in my pocket. It had the straight pin still attached, you know, so they can pin it to the garment. I stuck my finger with it and squeezed and squeezed until I had enough blood to write down just a couple of words, enough to jog my memory when I got back to civilization. What do you think of your crazy granddaughter?

P.S. Do you think Ramsey Smith is a boy or a girl?

Dearest Amy,

I spent some time rereading and thinking about your last letter. I took it to the orchard and sat under the flowering crabapple with the bees humming fat and lazy around my head.

It seems to me that you're talking about passion. You could be writing of your devotion to a man, such is the intensity of your description. This made me wonder where romantic love fits into your life? Or does it? I would be so very interested in hearing your thoughts on this.

Do you see Wayne in New York? You mentioned in passing that he works at the Natural History Museum, something to do with insects. The last time I saw the two of you in the same room together was here, last Christmas. Amy, darling, he does love you. It's quite clear in the way he gazes at you with such longing. It seems equally evident, however, that you don't return his ardor. Though by my count you do have four more years until your deadline.

And was there also someone named Kevin?

I wish you would tell me everything you can about your process of writing. I can't think of anything more interesting.

Love, Gran

Gran rarely mentioned the boyfriend issue. Amy knew it grieved her that she was unattached, and Amy had half jokingly assured her that she would visit the issue when she was thirty, a birthday that now loomed close on the horizon. The truth was, Amy wasn't so certain about falling in love. The closest she'd ever come was when she was fifteen, with Theo, the drug dealer. She still thought of him, in fact, which was alarming. What did that say about her? Both her mother and grandmother had suffered through marriages with troubled men. Amy had watched it, which was why she had pledged to herself that she would join a *convent* before she would carry on that particular tradition. Instead, she had vowed to throw her energy into writing; that producing a book would signal the end of something, and maybe the beginning as well. She would be free now, to explore all facets of her life—writing another book, certainly, and then another, but it was this one that proved a beloved tyrant in her head and in her heart.

26

Dear Gran,

Kevin is very good-looking. I'm so shallow anyway that, for the time being, just staring at him seems to keep me gratified enough.

Did I upset you with my gory tale? I never want *ever* to distress you in any way. How I wish we could be sitting side by side in the garden chairs to hash over such weighty issues as love and work and how to layer lasagna.

I remember one time when Mom and Dad went away and I stayed at your house. It was maybe my first sleepover because I was sad and a little scared. I must have been crying because you opened the door to the bedroom. You were backlit against the hall light with your hair cascading down your shoulders. You looked like an angel, and I remember feeling that nothing bad could ever happen to me. Now it's my turn to take care of you! I want to bring you tea and biscuits and make sure you're warm enough. I know how chilly you get on these cool spring nights with no fire in the fireplace.

You asked about writing. I've been keeping a journal. It's not secret, really, though it's very personal so there's no one but you whom I would share it with. When I'm writing, I often feel that I'm under a spell—I really question how much control over the process I have. Maybe after a few more years it won't feel quite so elusive. The journal is a way to pin it down, I suppose, to make writing more of a routine, like going to work in a factory each day. Of course, that's ridiculous, but I am so afraid that the slender golden thread attaching me to the world of imagination will suddenly tear and I'll never write again.

Just in case they are at all interesting, here are some excerpts from my journal. Sorry for the sloppy handwriting.

Today I went to a new doctor, so I was asked to fill out a form. I stared at the "Occupation" box for a long time. What am I if I'm not a writer? Am I a writer if I never publish a single word? I left it blank.

Writing is like being possessed. I can barely look or listen without thinking: how do I describe that? (The water lapping at the shore during a cold snap—is it viscous, sluggish, what?) I am constantly weighing my words, a walking Roget's.

My new heroine, Ellen O'Malley, is famous for being famous, empty at the core (we think, but she's really hiding). She drives through a traffic light and causes an accident in which someone dies because she does not believe that even traffic lights apply to her.

Sometimes I'm afraid I'll have some fatal accident before I finish the final draft of my book and someone will read it and think I thought this crap version was the finished product. The horror!

Along with the characters from my current book, there are people in my head from various projects, from other places, other centuries even. They exist apart from me, and I can tap into their lives at any time. This one is standing by the stove in the gaslight, stirring a pot, this one is walking on a mossy path in the woods accompanied by his three-legged dog. I can remember the people in stories I wrote as a child. Maybe this is why I rarely feel lonely. Miserable, fearful, yes, but not alone.

I had expected when I began the first novel that I would write exactly what I felt. Now I see that I can sometimes come achingly close, touch my finger briefly to the spot, especially at those inexplicable periods when the keyboard is clattering away faster than my thoughts and I'm just hanging on for dear life.

I like working in a small room, so that I can pluck the words out of the air before they can escape.

When I look back over these scribbles, Gran, I realize that I skirted around the piece of it that plagues me every day: my fear. I am almost always convinced that I will fail, that the cruel blank screen will win. That I have nothing important to say and that I'm living in delusion. I'm so intimidated by Mom's real-world accomplishments. She is making a difference in people's lives. I'm just a word whore. Maybe I should quit these ridiculous mutterings and get on with a productive occupation like teaching or going to medical school. These are the thoughts that torment me every day until *finally* I force myself to sit down and type a sentence. One sentence, which can be total nonsense—often is—and yet, for whatever reason, somehow that mechanical gesture starts the engine going and if I'm lucky, I'll have a decent day at the computer.

I'm so lucky to have you, Gran. You are my safe place.

Love, Amy

Dearest Amy,

I should have known you would remember that Saturday was the anniversary of Grandad's death and that I would be a little bit down in the dumps. Thank you for coming all the way up here in the pouring rain. Mercy, I half expected to see an ark floating past my window! And how dear that you would slog through the torrents with me to visit the cemetery. I am a lucky grandma indeed!

Today the sun shines in the rain-washed sky and I am cheerful.

Gratefully,
Gran

At this point her handwriting rapidly deteriorated, becoming wobbly and faint. But Amy continued to write regularly, unaware that this was Gran's final year.

27
Dear Gran,

For two weeks, it's been empty inside that place where my characters live. This has never happened to me before. Where is everybody?

Love from your freaked-out granddaughter,
Amy

Dearest Freaked-out,

Think of it this way: your imagination is a reservoir that never empties. When it's active, the spigot is open and ideas flood out. When it's closed, there's merely a drip, or perhaps nothing at all. But the deep water is merely still, waiting for the tap to open again. And it will. You'll see.

Love, Gran

(And the last, just a note jotted on a blank greeting card with a lily pictured on the front:)

27
Dear Gran,

You were right. It's deafening in here. I can't get them to shut up.

Love, Amy

Amy felt her throat thicken as she put the letters back inside and closed the box, and after sitting for so long, stood a little shakily. She folded up the tarp and set it down, laying her book on top. Then she walked to the car and opened the trunk. She removed a shovel and walked with it back to the gravesite. She lingered for a moment, breathing in the scent of new grass. She loved the way the trees looked in spring when the budding leaves veiled the trees in delicate pale green lace.

A lone golfer played up the center of the fairway nearby, striding with the loose long-legged gait of her grandfather. It seemed appropriate that he would visit her thoughts just now.

She dug a deep hole beside her grandmother's stone. Then she set the shovel down and retrieved her book. Amy imagined it lying beside her grandmother, the leaves on its cover murmuring, soothing. She opened the book carefully so as not to crack the binding. The print looked beautiful crossing the page, line after line. She held it open and cleared her throat.

"I got a good review in *Publisher's Weekly*, Gran. The reviewer said, and I quote, 'Vanderwall's novel is insightful, funny, poignant, not a new theme by any means, but deftly realized and altogether an auspicious debut.' What do you think of that?" She imagined Gran's face gazing back at her with pride and delight.

Amy listened to the silence for a moment. It was time. She knelt down on one knee, setting her book on the other. She took a pen from her pocket, held it poised for a moment above the title page, then began:

"For my dearest Gran. This book belongs to you. I would not be a writer if not for you. I would not be a *person* if not for you. You lit my way. You light it still."

And, because it felt like a prayer, she wrote:

"Amen."

MORE FROM SALLY MANDEL

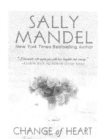

CHANGE OF HEART
Sometimes love is worth risking everything. A *New York Times* bestseller.

Sharlie Converse is twenty-six with a vivid and romantic interior life. Born with a heart defect that has defeated an army of specialists, she has lived her short life from moment to moment. Everything that matters most to her—color, excitement, adventure—is forbidden except in her imaginings and in the secret yearnings that she has long accepted will never be made real.

Until, on a cross town bus packed with Christmas shoppers, she falls into Brian Morgan's arms. And Sharlie, whom love can kill, must make the agonizing choice: to risk her life by loving or never really to live at all.

QUINN

An unlikely romance struggles in the face of dueling dreams.

Headstrong and beautiful Quinn Mallory makes the impulsive decision to offer herself as the first prize in a college contest. Will Ingraham applies in verse, and wins. Their personalities couldn't be more different, but a true love blossoms between them that, they believe, will last forever. Until Quinn's dreams of a career in the big city collide with Will's longing for a quiet life together in his Idaho home—leaving Quinn to choose between the life she wants and the man she loves, and neither choice feeling like the right one.

PORTRAIT OF A MARRIED WOMAN

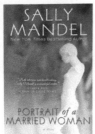

Dissatisfied in her life, a housewife returns to the passion she had put aside, and discovers a new one as well.

After seventeen years of marriage, Maggie Hollander should have it all. Her husband, Matthew, still loves her deeply, and two irrepressible children complete the picture-perfect family in their elegant New York apartment. But at thirty-eight, Maggie has questions about herself that grow deeper and more disturbing. Once a promising artist, she decides to return to art class in search of answers. It is there that she meets a sculptor who rekindles her talent, and her passion. David Golden will expose Maggie to a tenderness that is as liberating as it is dangerous, and will carry her toward an unforeseen choice.

OUT OF THE BLUE

A poignant and provocative romance about a remarkable leap of faith.

Anna Bolles is a born athlete whose life was irrevocably changed after a multiple sclerosis diagnosis five years ago. Anna fills her days with the vibrancy of life in New York City, teaching at a private school, but shutting the door on any possible romance. Until Joe Malone enters her life.

A businessman, pilot, and amateur photographer, Joe Malone has it all – except happiness. He sees far more in Anna than just her MS diagnosis, and takes Anna on a roller coaster of love, hope, and hanging on.

HEART AND SOUL

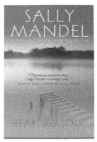

An undeniable talent is coaxed into the spotlight in a witty and tender romance.

Bess Stallone is brash and bold, until she is placed center stage. A self-taught musical prodigy from the rough side of Long Island, the only thing Bess has in common with her Juilliard classmates is her passion for classical music, and her extraordinary skill on the piano. A skill that crumbles under the weight of self-doubt when she plays for an audience.

Virtuoso David Montagnier is drawn to Bess's wild talent, and gives her the opportunity she's been waiting for to escape her blue-collar existence. He holds the key to Bess's dreams – and surprisingly, she may hold the key to his – if she will surrender to the music and believe in love.

CPSIA information can be obtained
at www.ICGtesting.com
Printed in the USA
FFHW02n1134090918
48253110-52020FF